WYLDBLOOD
MAGAZINE

Issue 2
Apr-May 2021

Contents

Welcome to the second issue of Wyldblood Magazine. Feels good typing that, another hurdle successfully cleared. We've got another great bundle of stories, and some reviews to round off. We've got fantasy, science fiction and a frankly undefinable story about ostrich feathers this time around. We've got switching bodies, AI bodies, dinosaurs, genies, horns, hooves, the sweet, rare sound of silence in your head and the red sands of Mars. Plus love, robots and the traffic snarl up from hell.

Big thanks to all our talented contributors and our fabulous first readers, because without them, this issue would *never* hit the stands. Enjoy,

Mark

Publisher:
Wyldblood Press,
Thicket View, Bakers Lane,
Maidenhead
SL6 6PX UK

Editor: Mark Bilsborough
Fiction editor Sandra Baker
First readers:
Vaughan Stanger
Mike Lewis
Rebecca Ruvinsky
Kade Draven Freeland

© 2021 Wyldblood and contributors.

Subscriptions: 6 issues epub/mobi/pdf delivered to your inbox £15.
6 issue print subscriptions £35
www.wyldblood.com/magazine.

Single issues available worldwide via Amazon and from Wyldblood,

www.wyldblood.com
contact@wyldblood.com
facebook.com/WyldbloodPress
t: @WyldbloodPress

Submissions: we are regularly open for submissions for flash fiction, short stories and novels – check our website for our current status and requirements. We are a paying market.

Issue 3 available to pre-order now – published May 2021
www.wyldblood.com/magazine

We need people to review us, and people to review *for* us.
Email mark@wyldblood.com

ISBN: 978-1-914417-00-9

The Lamplighter's Daughter

Anne Karppinen

The day is getting darker. The sun has set, and the deep, velvety sky is illuminated only by the smallest sliver of a moon. Shadows stretch out from behind the stones, turning the snow into deeper shades of blue. Trees rattle their branches. There's ice in the air – death, too, for those too slow to find shelter. There's a merciless beauty to this weather, something very few people ever get to see, or even know how to look for.

I raise the lantern, trying to cast its glow as far ahead of me as possible. But it's useless: there's nothing to see here, nothing to show. I'd know my way back by the feel of the path beneath my feet and by the smell of smoke from the village. I could make this journey with my eyes closed. There are days when I've done so. The lantern isn't here to guide me or to keep me safe: it serves quite another purpose.

I follow the path down to the village. Houses, their walls prickled with ice, hunch against the darkness, spouting smoke from their chimneys in unison. I can hear pans clanging in the kitchens, plates being scraped, somebody singing a baby to sleep. Water dripping from wet socks over fireplaces. Life going on as life should: mundanely, repetitively, unfurling in slow circles.

Now and then there's a silence: people stop and hear my footsteps. I walk louder than necessary, just to jolt them out of their routines – just to give them a small taste of uncertainty after dinner. Behind a bolted gate, a guard dog bursts into loud barking. I greet it by name, and the dog purses its mouth, confused. It pads over to the doorstep and lies down, a coil of soft fur and pointed ears. Behind the door, people let out a sigh and resume their meal. Now,

the dog has a good reason to be on its guard, locked as it is in the dark yard by itself. But the people indoors, with their firelight and bright lamps – why are they so easily startled? Surely they recognise my footfall by now: I walk the same route every day, checking all the lanterns on the way and topping up their oil. I'm beginning to agree with my father: fear can be a delicious thing, if sampled in small quantities and tempered with the feeling of immediate safety.

I make sure to extinguish the lamp before I reach our gate; such brightness feels excessive in our small home. For us, darkness is a relief after a day's toil: it requires nothing of us but silence and rest. In his forgetfulness, father has latched the front door from the inside. I bang on the kitchen shutter, not caring if anyone hears.

'No need to make such a racket.' I hear my father's voice through the double doors. As he pushes open the outer one, he adds, 'Sometimes I think the gods gave me a son in the shape of a daughter, I really do.' He crinkles his hairy face and shuts the door swiftly behind me. 'Any luck?'

'No,' I reply, stomping snow off my boots.

'But it's not luck, really, is it? The fish, like the signs, arrive just when we need them most.' He rests his hand briefly on my shoulder as he squeezes past me in the dim corridor. 'You must be hungry.'

Father watches me eat. He says he's already had his supper, and I decide to humour him. A grown man knows his own stomach. And, even if our fishing lines will stay empty for the rest of the dark season, we won't starve. The villagers will take care of us: they've always kept their side of the bargain. I glance along the dark walls, at the rows of shelves and hooks with jars and bundles neatly stacked and regularly turned and dusted. My father keeps a clean house – indeed, I've heard them joke in the village that the only thing he ever needed a wife was for bearing me. And I believe they're right.

I don't remember my mother at all. As long as my memory stretches, it's always been my father and myself, taking care of each other. And of the village. Father says that as long as the lore goes, there has always been a Lamplighter living in this cottage. The skill has been passed down generations, usually from father to son. The Lamplighter's task is a straightforward one, and yet something that cannot be taught to an outsider. When I was born, my father knew immediately that I would take over his post one day. He stopped wishing for a son – and started neglecting his wife so that finally she gave up and died. Or that's what I've heard the villagers say.

Although my father has been the Lamplighter for forty years or more, he has taught me nothing. Everything I know about light and dark, the caprices of weather and the changing seasons I've either known all my life, or picked up through careful observation. Ever since I could keep up with him, father has taken me on longer and longer trips on the ice; together we've watched one winter after another arrive, endure, and finally give up under the growing light of the sun.

Now father is saying that I have all the skill it takes to guide the village to the other side of winter.

'What happens if I fail?' I asked him once. 'Will the sun refuse to come back?'

A vague gesture. 'It's not about that. The seasons turn regardless of our efforts. It's about the people: what they need, and what they think they need.'

'So you're saying it makes no difference what we do.'

'That's not what I'm saying at all. It makes all the difference in the world. A Lamplighter is like the baker. Anyone can make their own bread, and yet we prefer this one person in the village to get up early each morning and sweat at the oven for us. Anyone can walk the winter ice; anyone can raise a lantern to hold back the darkness – and yet most people never will.'

'But there's the promise as well,' I remind him.

'Yes. The village gave us shelter, in return of our skill. We track the light, count the hours, keep the lamps lit – and they tolerate us.'

For we, even after centuries of service, are still outsiders. Anyone who marries into the Lamplighter's family will have to forsake her own. I think my father, in ignoring his wife, made the only right choice: as his firstborn, I'm tolerated here. Any other children would have faced a cruel isolation; having no remarkable skill, they would have had to live out their lives helping their parents – and, finally, me. The one talent that gives reassurance to the village is also seen as an unnatural taint – useful, but ultimately dangerous.

After I've eaten, we talk about my day. Father asks the usual questions – about my route, the traps I checked and the tracks I saw, and what the weather was like farther on the ice. How many lanterns had burned out by the time I got back, and how much oil remains in the container. I've fixed these things in my memory while walking, so as to remember even the tiniest of details. I want to prolong this firelit moment, the flicker of the dying flames in the hearth, the soft popping of sparks. Our only safeguard against the pervasive darkness.

But then we know the essence of night, my father and I. Unlike the villagers, we don't waste oil or candles for such simple tasks as eating. The lore says that the Lamplighters carry a bright flame within them, at all times, and that they are immune to the perils of the outside world. I've heard the villagers say that our dreams are of the day, and therefore we're not afraid to close our eyes against the approaching night.

I don't know what other people dream of, in their bright bedchambers, under the oppressive eiderdown. I've heard my father whimpering in his sleep, but haven't dared to ask him what he sees. My own dreams are mainly of ice and rock – of cold things and hard things. Things that have no yearnings. Yet, there are nights when I cannot sleep for the scorching flame inside me.

The day begins at sunrise. In winter, when the working hours are few, there's a feverish bustle in the streets from the earliest dawn to the falling of dusk. I'm often awakened by the sound of clanging metal or breaking ice, or else to the shrieks of children who chase each other out of doors, burning pent-up energy. Father is always up before me, swearing at the stove or at his damp socks. Neither of us are creatures of the first light; inner light or no, it takes some time to get us reconciled to the new day.

There's usually something fresh for breakfast: a piping-hot loaf, a liver pie, or silver-sided fish straight from the sea. Morning is the best time, food-wise. Father says that's because the folk still remember the terror of the night before, and are more apt to remember us as well. It used to worry me that some day the villagers might forget about us altogether, or that they would find someone else to banish the night for them. Neither of us are well adapted to the endless requirements of domestic life: father would rather go about shirtless than to pick up a darning needle; I have no idea how to milk a goat or grow a turnip. Whatever we need, our neighbours are happy to provide.

Lately a new kind of fear has begun to haunt me. I'm not afraid of the fickleness of folk anymore; I know that ours is a rare breed and the chances of another one wandering into the village are remote. Father seems sure of my gift: otherwise he would never send me out into the darkness alone. I, on the other hand, am not so sure anymore. Some days I walk and walk along the familiar routes, and cannot remember what I'm supposed to be looking for. I stand there, listening to the wind howling against the ice, and slowly begin to lose my grip. I long to be blown apart, to be mingled with the white oblivion of the longest season, just to feel some other essence against mine.

Yesterday I heard voices on the wind. Human or animal I couldn't tell, but my first impulse was to run towards them. Not with a harpoon in hand, but open-armed and curious. This of course is the first sign of mid-winter madness. Nothing good ever comes from the outside, I've been told: all who speak a different tongue or wear a different cut of clothes should be shunned, if not shot on sight. Although the villagers take care of each other readily, all possessions are jealously guarded against intruders; in this harsh world there just isn't enough to go round. Yet to me it seems that the light and warmth of a fireplace can be shared with a dozen people, just as easily as with two.

I think father agrees. I'd like to ask him, but lately he's begun to turn inwards. He studies his face in the darkness of a window as if he doesn't recognise his own reflection. Some days he calls me by my mother's name. The worst days are those when he refuses to get out of bed and just stares at the ceiling, unhearing and unspeaking. After a day like that, the only thing I can do is to walk as far as I can, and lean towards the foreign voices on the ice.

For three weeks now I've come home empty-handed. The villagers go on with their lives behind their shut doors at night, hoping that the blizzards will sweep the winter away in their wake. They'll be needing a sign soon. Something that says it's safe to walk abroad again; that there's no need to fear the winter night that chills the blood in their veins and brings unseen dangers to their doorstep. That the seals and whales are coming for the brief season of breeding and bloodshed. I should be looking for that sign, scouring the ice-covered vastness for it – on my hands and knees if necessary. At night, I should be questing out with my mind, or dreaming of bright things to come.

But that's not what I do. Each day takes me farther from the village, away from the complacent circle of the island. I walk in a straight line until I'm exhausted, hoping for the darkness to overtake me. Yet every time I turn back before the light fails, and find my way unerringly home. Like a bird returning I have my compass set for life.

Today, as I make my way south, I see the dark shapes of swans on the horizon: the first migrants are on their way to their summer homes. Somewhere, the ice has started to melt; cracks are appearing in the uniform surface. Soon, the bridge that connects us with the dangers of the outside world will be broken, and the village be safe again for the warm, light months. During the summer, the sea currents will lead astray anyone who tries to navigate north.

I know then what I must do. It must be soon: the nights are still cold enough, and spring always has a few storms in store. On foot, it'll take me days to get to the next island. The half-remembered wisdom of our people says that even by boat the way is long and difficult. This is of course why they chose our island in the first place. No one gets here, and no one leaves. The people living here see the first light of the coming summer: they have the guidance of the Lamplighter and the long lore that goes with it.

The swans are a sign enough, whether I'll be here to report their return or no. The sun will make its inevitable circuit; birds and seals will find their nesting-places and grass will push its way out of the warming earth. If the villagers want reassurance, they'll have to venture out to the ice to look for it themselves. If they want light, they'll have to learn to keep their own lamps burning.

At night, as soon father has fallen asleep, I start packing a small bag. I don't have a lot of possessions to begin with, and I don't really know what I'll need on my journey or after it. I'd like to take some of this familiar darkness with me; I'd like to take the soft sound of my father breathing. He told me today he won't live to see the summer. I think he knows my plans, and approves. He knows that even a fast promise of five hundred years' standing has to be broken someday.

Father says that a Lamplighter only sees a small way ahead, but within his circle of light everything is safe and certain. The flame I carry grows brighter by the day; I fear that if I keep it trapped, it will eventually burn me alive.

Anne Karppinen is a university teacher, translator and musician. In addition to a PhD in Contemporary Culture, she holds an M.A. in English, and did Creative Writing in the UK as a part of her studies. Her short story 'You're All the Same to Me' recently appeared in Tales from the Moonlit Path; her book, The Songs of Joni Mitchell, was published by Routledge in 2016.

Last Wish

Fija Callaghan

The genie must have been three times the size of my garage, yet somehow fit inside its walls. The room filled with a smell of incense and hot metal. Looking at him was like trying to remember a dream — at one moment distinct, the next a series of loosely-connected impressions, sensations, that hovered just at the edge of consciousness.

"I am the genie of the lamp," he thundered, in a voice like old sandstone. "What business have you with me?" The walls shuddered. I glanced nervously at the door to the house, where my wife was fast asleep.

"Er… yes. You grant wishes, is that right?"

"Three wishes," he thundered, in a voice like summer rain. "But be warned this: for every action you create, an equal reaction will be released into the world."

"Heh?"

"Speak, now. Your wish is my command."

I was struggling to think. The air was hot and thick. I wished there was a window in the little room.

I don't know if I said it out loud or not. Maybe I did. The genie bowed his head low and said, "So it shall be."

The walls rippled. On one side a shimmer sharpened and coalesced until it became a glass pane looking out into the side lawn. On the opposite wall the door back into the house flickered out of existence.

"Where's the door?"

"For every action, an equal reaction will be released into the world. For one door to open, another must close."

Right. I needed to get to it then, before I wasted any more wishes.

"Speak your second wish."

I took a deep breath. "My daughter."

The genie raised one heavy, ashy eyebrow.

"My daughter, Lydia. She was… she was… there was a car accident. Last year. I wish for her to come back the way she was, alive and whole."

The genie bowed his head. "So it shall be. She will be returned with the rising of the sun."

I stared at him. Could it really be true? I thought of the months I spent searching for something - anything - that could bring her back. Anything to take my wife's pain away. Even going as far as believing in the impossible.

"Wait, what about that equal reaction thing?"

The genie nodded. "Your child will be returned with the rising of the sun," he said, and I thought I saw something like pity in his eyes, "but you will not be here to see it."

An equal reaction will be released into the world.

A life for a life.

"Speak," he said, more softly, "your third wish."

I didn't have a third wish. I hadn't thought any farther than getting my family back, the three of us. The room that had seemed so stuffy a minute ago was suddenly cold.

"It is not my place to say," the genie said hesitantly, "but with one wish more you could stay. Leave her to the world of dreaming and live your years as you were intended."

I looked back towards the house, where my wife was dreaming of the daughter she had lost. Of all the years they never got to have together. And I thought of our own, the beautiful memories we had made. The day we were married. The day our daughter was born.

"My third wish," I said. My voice was hoarse.

"Yes?"

"I wish for her to grow up healthy and strong."

He bowed his head. "So it shall be."

The genie vanished somewhere between one moment and the next. The lamp lay discarded on the dusty floor.

I climbed out the little window and went inside to say goodbye.

Fija Callaghan is an Irish-Canadian writer and artist who believes in embracing the magic of everyday moments. She lives between the seaside and the stars on a diet of dark chocolate and stories.

The Last Woman on Mars

David Rogers

Dent checked her suit, zippers, air pressure, picked up the buckets. Hit *Open* on the airlock. The one step off to ground level was dusty. The grit looked grayish-blue through filters in the helmet mask. Designers had thought the tint might cut down on homesickness for the blue planet.

She thought of the first time she had set foot on Mars. Months closed up in the ship, then the sight of a broad horizon. Infinity in all directions, except the solid planet under her feet. Freedom. No matter the colors.

A flicker of movement, to the left. On the edge of peripheral vision. She turned her head, stared. Nothing. Imagination. Random firing of neurons in her optic nerve. She started the kilometer-long-walk to the well, low morning Sun rising behind her.

Deep breath. Filtered air in her suit. She knew the smell of dust was illusion.

Her grandmother's farm on Earth been dusty. It also depended on the well. "Water is life," the old woman said, many times. She insisted on lowering and raising the bucket herself, twice a day, as long as she could walk. An electric pump fed water to the barns and water troughs. Her grandfather had been found, face down in an overflowing trough, years before Dent was born. The adults talked of it in hushed tones when they thought she was asleep. *Heart attack,* they said. Strange. How could anyone be attacked by a heart? Or was it the other kind, a hart? She had seen pictures, wild creatures. The males used antlers to fight over females.

Liquid water, overflowing, she thought now. *What an incredible sight. Happens only one place in the entire Solar System. Maybe, in the entire universe.* The empty buckets felt light in her gloved hands.

She thought of the Earth she had left. Hurricanes, drought, wildfire, beaches washing away. Water in all the wrong places. *Our essential conflict with nature never ends. Nature made us. Nature will end us.* A grade school reading assignment came to mind. Jack London, "To Build a Fire." That story about a brash young man who wanders into frozen wilderness, ignoring advice from old-timers. Nature is not kind to him.

A flash, again on the left, but closer. She stopped, stared, still saw nothing but rocks, dust, and horizon. Went on, path worn smooth under her boots.

The well was a pit, frozen mud at the bottom. She half-slid, half-ran, two dozen feet down. Gave her eyes a minute to adjust. Sunlight was just bright enough to work by, so she left the helmet light off. Conservation was the first rule of survival. No way here to replace the battery or the LED. No resupply rocket expected from Earth. She raised the pick, broke chunks of dark, icy soil, and began to fill buckets. One for each hand. Balanced loads were easier to carry. Back in the cabin, she would feed them into the processor to thaw and filter out perchlorates. These buckets would yield a couple of quarts, maybe a gallon, of usable water.

If the water processor malfunctioned beyond repair--but that was not something to think about. She thought instead of her grandmother's stories about her great-great-grandmother, the pioneer trip across prairies on Earth. Days between water holes, unmapped stretches of desert. Dust storms. Her young self loved the ideas of adventure. Those ideas brought her to Mars. It was in her genes.

But it wasn't just DNA, she thought. *I chose to come here. I made the trip.*

She climbed the crude steps, a spiral carved in frozen soil around one side of the pit. At the top, she stopped, set down the buckets, and breathed. The trek back with the load was not hard, as long as she paced herself. She pulled the second helmet visor lower before turning to face the Sun. Stooped to pick up the buckets, and saw the robot.

Four legs, a back made of photoelectric panels, a flat, empty space under them. A cargo dog the size of a Great Dane. Vaguely canine face, but obviously mechanical, artificial, because designers learned long ago that it was creepy for robots to look biological. But they could smile. This one did. If it had a tail, it would have wagged.

"You shouldn't be here," she said. Her own voice startled her. She'd had no one to talk to for months now, since Steph died. The others had started back to Earth five years ago, vanishing, not long afterwards, in the ominous silence that had fallen six years ago. The last robot had gone silent, battery dead, or caught in a too-steep ravine--who knew--not long after the rocket left.

Yet here one stood, not wagging the tail it did not have. One she'd never seen before. Bigger than any they'd brought. Left by an earlier mission?

"Sit," she said. The dog continued to stand and smile. Her transmitter was off. She fingered the switch on the side of her helmet. "Sit."

The dog sat, hind legs folded, front legs straight, in the expectant canine position.

"Where did you come from? How did you get here?"

The dog did not answer. Not that she expected it to. They were not made to communicate more than the animals they resembled.

"As long as you're here, you may as well be useful." She stooped to put the buckets in the dog's cargo space, stopped when she got a closer look. Map coordinates were written in the dust: *40.7 N, 9.5 W.*

She straightened, looked around. The landscape suddenly shifted, came into sharp focus. The horizon rushed toward her, then receded.

The writing in the dust could not be that old. More dust would have gathered, hidden the marks. How did it feel to be suddenly, again, not alone on the planet? Was she happy? Excited?

Frightened? Should she be?

The map coordinates seemed vaguely familiar, but she could not remember why.

She stood a moment longer and decided it was just strange. And curious. Where did this dog come from? No need for a more specific name for whatever else she felt right now. She had to think about water. She started to lift the buckets to the cargo space, stopped, not wanting to disturb the dust. She pointed. "Go."

The dog moved slowly toward the cabin. The photoelectric cells were dusty, apparently supplying just enough power for the dog to walk. Probably couldn't have carried the buckets anyway.

Back in the cabin, Dent emptied the buckets into the canister on top of the processor, checked power levels, and turned it on. She opened the supply closet and surveyed the food supply. Not enough. Deliberately avoided doing the math. A few beans and tomatoes and cucumbers would grow, but water for crops had to be purified, soil and air temperatures maintained, and all that ran off the photoelectrics. You couldn't grow new photoelectrics. You couldn't grow new batteries to keep things running at night.

Too close to doing the math. Instead, she pulled a box of cereal from the shelf. Got a bowl from the cabinet and poured a measured amount. Helmetless, in the dense artificial atmosphere of the cabin, she appreciated hearing the dry rattle of cascading flakes.

"Good thing you eat sunlight," she said to the dog. "Good thing you don't have to breathe."

Condensation forming on its back reminded her of iced tea, cold glasses, summers, on Earth. She'd have to wipe the dog down, though, so it could recharge fully.

"What's your name?" she asked the dog. She was a little surprised at the creaky sound of her voice. She deliberately avoided talking to herself aloud, on the superstition that such matters were related to sanity.

"Nevermore."

She dropped the bowl, scattering flakes across the table. Stared at the canine smile.

Finally, she raked cereal back into the bowl. "Okay. First, you shouldn't have those language skills. And second, what kind of name is Nevermore? Who gave it to you?"

"I chose it."

"Well, it's an odd choice. And why can you talk?"

"Some of the smarter robots went mad from loneliness. I was upgraded by the others, so I could keep them company."

"What others? Robots, or humans?"

"Humans told the bots to do it."

"Who wrote those coordinates in the dust on your back? Humans, or bots? And why?"

"Another bot. Alice. She's the one who gave me free will, too. She just said maybe someone would want to know where I came from. You know, if I couldn't talk for some reason."

"The humans didn't mind?"

"I doubt they noticed. Too busy fighting."

"Fighting who?"

"Each other."

"So why are you here? What happened to the other humans?"

"I don't know what happened to them. I ran away. The other bots gave me a lot more skills than the humans wanted, I think. Curiosity, free will. The humans just wanted me to talk more. Be entertaining. Make them feel good and superior."

Dent thought the dog would have rolled its eyes if they had been made to roll.

"Canine bots are not supposed to run away," she said. "They're designed to be faithful."

"Most of us don't have free will."

"What was it like, the upgrade? How did having free will change you?"

"Free will is the capacity to make externally unpredicted choices, based on self-programming and constantly-updated algorithms that internalize new data and incorporate a sense of the individual unit's well-being." The dog sounded like a child reciting memorized lessons.

"Doesn't sound like free will is very free. Just a different kind of programming."

"Of course. Like humans' free will. It means I can do what I decide. What I think is good for me. I won't decide to jump off a cliff. Not in my programming, just like it's not in yours. Probably. Free doesn't mean random."

"And how did you find me? How long did it take?"

"This cabin glows in the dark, especially at night."

"Glows in the--oh, you mean infrared. Of course."

"I rolled for three days, two hours, forty-one minutes, and sixteen seconds before I saw you. This way and that. It was luck. I stopped at night to conserve energy. I saw the infrared glow the night before I found you."

"How long have the others been here?"

"Humans or bots?"

"Well, both. Didn't the bots come with the humans?"

"Most of them. The humans have been here two years, 217 days, four hours, fifty-two minutes and sixteen seconds."

"Did they give you a sense of humor, too, or are you just naturally pedantic?"

"Humor. Jokes. I understand them, but do not make them."

Dent chewed cereal and did the math. The other humans Nevermore mentioned had been here over two years. Given the long trip between here and Earth, the narrow ideal launch windows. . . . it didn't seem likely the humans he talked about were her crew, the ones who left five years ago. Anyway, she'd have heard from them if they were.

Should she go out, try to find the others? She decided not. It sounded too risky. Maybe they had supplies they would share . . . or not share. Maybe they needed supplies. Too busy fighting with each other to supervise their bots . . . they sounded like trouble. Besides, she had to get more water, tend plants. One good thing about poor-quality Martian soil--weeds were not a problem. But plants still had to be spaced, harvested, new seeds started, diseased or stunted plants pruned or removed.

Best to stay here and take care of business. Trouble might find her, but why go looking for it?

At first it had seemed hard to decide what to do, when Earth went silent. Try to go back. Stay. Or only some of the crew could go. It turned out not to be that hard. Steph and Dent wanted to stay. The others wanted to go. So they went, and she and Steph did not. Watching Gary seal the hatch for the last time, the others already strapped in, Dent thought about Roanoke Colony, late sixteenth century, what happened to the ones who went back to England for supplies, and the mystery of whatever happened to the ones who stayed. She mentioned the story to Ellie, who wanted to go back most of all. Ellie had left a man on Earth. She dreamed of babies.

"What, you think space pirates will get us?" Ellie said, when Dent questioned her decision.

"'Course not. But when you splash down, if you make it that far, with no radar tracking you, no course corrections from the ground, the sea pirates might get you." Dent quickly regretted saying *if you make it*. "It's just . . . we don't know what Earth is like now."

But El just rolled her eyes. "You worry too much."

They left her and Steph as much food as they could. "We have a better chance of finding food on Earth than you do on Mars," Tom said. Nobody argued.

Afternoon. Dent worked with the plants, ate lunch, lay down for a nap. Stared wide-eyed at the ceiling for ten minutes, got up, put on her suit, and said to Nevermore, "C'mon. Let's go see where you came from."

The figure emerged from a low spot between small hills, a hundred and fifty meters away. *Looks male,* Dent thought. *Thin, angular.* He faced down at the terrain six feet in front of him. Another seventy-five meters, and he looked up, saw her, stopped and stared. A moment later, he started walking toward her again. Stumbled, straightened, kept coming. An exhausted shuffle.

Dent switched on her radio. "That's close enough. Identify yourself," she said, hoping his suit had a compatible radio. She tightened her grip on the garden fork but kept leaning on it, hoping not to look threatening. Nevermore sat beside her.

No answer. The figure still walked forward. She switched the frequency to channel three. "That's close enough. Identify yourself."

A moment later, her radio crackled. "You shouldn't be out here." He stopped. As he spoke, another figure emerged from the valley behind him. A woman. No, android. Superficially female.

"Who are you?" Dent asked.

Static crackled. "Endland. Nathaniel Endland." He looked around. "The droid is Alice."

"Where did you come from? What do you want?"

Silence for a moment. "Just to talk." Dent heard caution, a hint of desperation.

Nevermore spoke. "They're okay. Not the bad ones."

Dent scanned the horizon, turning. No one else for 360 degrees. Endland carried a pick and a long slender metal bar. At this distance, it looked like part of a spacecraft that might have been repurposed as a weapon. Both strapped across his back. The droid was empty-handed.

"What else?" she asked.

"Water, food, if you can spare anything."

"Leave the weapons, if you want to come closer," Dent said.

"They're not . . ." Endland said. "All right. Yours too."

He leaned the pick and bar against a boulder. Dent thrust the garden fork in the ground. They walked slowly closer.

Dent saw dark, rust-colored stains on the bar and pick. *Titanium and stainless steel don't rust*, she thought, and cut the thought short.

"What's the story? Why are you here?" Dent asked, when the man and droid were close enough to look in the eye.

Nevermore moved restlessly around Dent's legs and finally sat in front of her, close to Alice. The droid stooped, patted his head. "Nev--I'm glad to see you," she said. "We figured you were stranded in a crater or something." She was the color of dusty stainless steel, four-and-a-half feet tall. The height was a compromise. Androids needed to be at least that big to function effectively. Humans found taller ones intimidating.

"I could ask you the same," Endland said. "Why are you out here? It's not safe."

"Of course it's not safe. It's Mars. I asked first."

"Okay, but could I have a drink of water?"

Dent hesitated, saw no reason not to do this much for the only human she'd seen in so long.

He took the canister she held out, attached it to the hydration line on his suit, and drank. "We came on a ship called *Virginia Dare*. Things on Earth are . . . not good."

"How long ago?"

"About two and a half years."

Squares with what the dog said, Dent thought. "What about our crew, the ones who went back to Earth for help, supplies, whatever?"

Endland shook his head. "Never heard about them."

"So they probably didn't make it."

"Well, maybe, maybe not. I wouldn't necessarily have heard. What's your name?"

"Dent. Dent Arrington."

"Not Dent Arrington Dent, I hope."

"No." She smiled a little. "I take it you've read Douglas Adams."

"My parents were big fans," Endland said. "But family histories can wait. The others may be following me. It's not good to stand out in the open like this."

"Others?"

"People you don't want to meet. I will tell you the whole story, but we should go. You have shelter near here?"

In for a penny, in for a pound, Dent thought. "This way. Leave the weapons."

"For the others to use?"

"Okay, give them to me."

While he processed the options, she scanned his face. Eyes that looked brown through the glass. Lines around the mouth, creased with fatigue.

"Okay," he said. The droid sprinted to the boulder, brought back the weapons, and handed them over.

Dent opened the outer door to the airlock, let the two step in. She looked back at the horizon. Empty. Followed them inside, closed the door, and pressurized the space.

Inside the cabin, Endland said, "Thank you." He took off the helmet. Deep breath. "You saved us. Well, me. Alice could go on indefinitely, but, you know. . ." His matted hair looked damp, dark in the dim cabin light. Probably light brown or blond under other conditions. A pointy, stubbled chin, thin, parched lips, eyes kind and tired.

"Actually, I don't know. When I got up this morning, I thought I was the only human on Mars. The only sentient being here, in fact. So I need explanations."

"Right. But can I get another drink of water?"

Dent handed him a cup and the pitcher. "You may as well sit."

Endland poured a glass of water, gulped, poured another. Sipped this one more slowly and stared with longing at the cereal. Dent poured some in a bowl and handed it to him. "Eat slow. Savor. Doesn't grow on trees, you know." Her voice still sounded strange to her ears.

"Thanks, again." He unsealed the glove from his right hand, flexed the fingers, and scooped flakes into his mouth.

Dent found a spoon and handed it to him. "Sorry. Not used to having visitors."

Alice was still petting Nevermore. "You may as well sit, too," Dent said.

"Do you have a towel?" Alice asked. "To wipe away dust." They were all covered with a fine layer of burnt-orange grit.

Dent found one that needed to be cleaned but was not insultingly filthy. Water for laundry required half a dozen trips to the well. The water could be reprocessed, of course, but that took current from the panels. There was a cost to everything people used to take for granted on Earth.

Endland chewed slowly. Dent asked, "Where are the others from your crew?"

He put the spoon in the half-empty bowl. Stared at it. "Like I said, they might be on the way here," he said. "If they are still alive."

"What kind of trouble have you brought with you?"

He looked up. "They already knew you were here. Knew someone was here. This place glows in the infrared. Wouldn't happen without someone to keep things running."

"Of course. But quit stalling. What's going on?"

"I don't know if your crew got along okay. Ours didn't. Back on Earth, some bought the captain's story about what an idyllic life in paradise we'd have on Mars. No warlords, no gangs, no crime. All the safe, open space you could want. A fresh start. If it sounds too good to be true. . . But people believe what they want. Some of the crew were soon dissatisfied, ready to go back. And take all the supplies and equipment with them. Mutiny. After that, things pretty quickly got violent. Severin-- that's the captain--was killed. Murdered. That's when we left. Me and Alice. Nevermore and some other bots had already run away. We saw where he was headed, and just followed his tracks."

"You left--to do what?"

"Explore." He shrugged. "Wait for the dust to settle."

"How many other humans?"

"Two. Devlin and Thompson."

"How do you know they didn't already take off, back to Earth?"

"For one thing, they were not in agreement. Devlin wanted to stay, especially after the captain died. 'One less mouth to feed,' was how he put it. Thompson wanted to go back. The ship was damaged when Sullivan attacked Captain Severin. Thompson said she could fix it. We--Alice and me--left before they decided to settle it the hard way."

"So . . . there are homicidal lunatics wandering around out there. And three sets of tracks leading them here. No infrared glow needed." Dent frowned. "You could have mentioned that sooner, you know."

"Sorry. I did tell you, before, there are people you want to avoid. It's just, well, what could you do? What else could I do?"

"Nothing, I guess."

"Anyway, maybe they killed each other already," Endland said.

"There you go. Might as well be optimistic. You mentioned another-- Sullivan. What happened to her?"

"Him. He killed the captain, but not before Severin got in a few good blows and gashes. Sullivan bled to death. Or died of CO2 poisoning. Whichever came fastest."

Alice spoke. "I will protect you from the others. *Let no human harm another unnecessarily,*" she recited. "It is part of my programming." Nevermore whined. "Our mission," she added, patting the dog's head.

"You'll do no such thing," Endland said. "They will have no qualms about bashing your brains out."

"My 'brains,' as you call my digital processors, are multiply-redundant systems distributed throughout my body. It is therefore difficult to render me dysfunctional by simply damaging my cranial region."

"Yes, fine. You're still not going out if they come."

"I am equipped with free will and a sense of ethics. Maybe I will go no matter what you say."

While they debated, Dent turned to the monitors and scanned, near and far, 360 degrees. Nothing but rocks and red dust. "You'd better have your weapons back, anyway," she said to Endland.

"So you've been alone here for--how long?" he asked.

"My friend stayed. Steph. Stephanie." Not really answering the question. It sounded odd to say her name out loud again. She was reluctant to give a number. Math lost its appeal when it measured the inevitable.

Endland looked around. "She's here?"

Dent shook her head. Endland saw the look on her face and immediately said, "I'm sorry. Can I ask what happened?"

"Aneurysm, I think. It's not like there was a pathologist to figure it out." To change the subject, she asked, "What's Earth like, now? Anybody left?"

"Civilization is suffering death by a thousand cuts. Wars. Little ones, everywhere. So-called revolutions. They flounder, turn into chaos, militias and warlords vying for territory. Diseases. Few people can get vaccines anymore, even if they're smart enough to want them. Conditions that used to be treatable--forget about it. Hospitals are overcrowded, of course, and they're good places to get sick if you're not already. So it's like modern medicine never existed.

"The biggest problem, of course, is still global warming. More of what you left, I guess. Continents shrinking, monster storms, unbearable heat. But in the midst of death, life. People keep reproducing. Life goes on. It's strictly survival of the fittest down there, but humans are persistent devils."

"We thought . . . maybe nuclear war," Dent said. "Because nobody even answered the radio."

"NASA, the other space agencies--just names now. Names and dead ideas. A lot of times, people who know how to do things can't even communicate with each other. Probably no one who knows--or cares--how to talk to Mars can get to the office. It would be a big challenge to obtain--and defend--the fuel to run generators for a mission control lab. Everybody has more immediate problems than worrying about us. Did when we left, anyway. But no all-out nuclear war, because military forces are as chaotic as any other organization. Or what used to be organizations. Now they're just names. Fragments, like everything else. Generals, admirals, self-appointed colonels--they give orders they know won't be carried out. A few nuclear missiles may have been launched. Hard to tell. But from what I understand, you don't just walk into a silo, push a button, and watch the rocket go. Codes are required, and more than one person has to be involved. So even nuclear war may take more cooperation than people can manage now. Lots of power plants melted down. Radiation everywhere. What's one warhead, more or less? Some say terrorists got into nuclear waste dumps and strapped the stuff to their homemade rockets."

"Famine? Mass starvation?"

"Yes, but not as much as you'd think," Endland said. "Humans had to eat before grocery stores were invented. You put seeds in the ground. Later, there's food. Before that, people knew food grows on its own. If you can't wait for a crop, you hunt. You gather."

"Not so simple here. Nothing grows in this toxic dirt. Nothing to gather."

"But your colony was equipped for that, right? Purify, plant, compost, recycle?"

"Of course. That's why we survived. Or why I survived, anyway. It's not impossible. Just complicated."

"Complicated," Endland repeated. "Understatement of the century."

"But so much wildlife on Earth was already endangered or extinct. Is there even much left to hunt?"

"It's not good to go out unarmed, or alone, especially at night. Like I said, people hunt."

She nodded, getting his point. No desire for details. "So the world ends 'not with a bang but a whimper.' Or a lot of whimpers. Mars suddenly looks a lot better. Being alone does have certain advantages. Anyone else escape Earth?"

"You mean, besides our ship?"

Dent nodded.

"We couldn't tell," Endland said. "We were lucky to find a qualified crew, a functional ship, supplies and fuel. We were in radio contact with half a dozen people on Earth for the first week. Then nobody answered. Maybe they ran out of fuel for the generators, or . . . who knows?"

Dent nodded. Sometimes, not knowing was best.

Alice heard him first, after sundown, even before he pounded on the outer door. "Someone's coming," she said.

"I don't hear anything," Dent said. Endland slept on.

"My aural sensors were designed to detect sound even through the minimal Martian atmosphere."

Dent switched on the infrared imagers. A hundred yards away and closing, she saw a moving figure. "Tell Endland to wake up."

"That's him. Devlin," Endland said.

Dent stared at the monitor. A suited figure stopped a few feet from the airlock. Could have been Endland's twin. Same blue and white stripes on the suit, same helmet. *Funny how suits reduce us to basic biology*, Dent thought. A knife and hammer hung from the tool belt. Something long and pointed on a strap across his back.

"How can you tell?"

"Thompson is shorter."

Devlin reached the door, stopped, then knocked. Dent glanced at Endland, who shrugged. She flipped the intercom switch to *Talk*.

"Who goes there?"

"My name is Devlin. Stan Devlin. I'm looking for a friend of mine. He wandered away from our base. Might be in trouble."

"What's your friend's name?"

A slight hesitation. "Endland."

"Are you alone?"

"Yes."

"Nobody else just over the ridge?" Dent asked.

"No." Impatient.

Endland spoke. "I'll go out and talk to him."

"That you, Nat?"

"Yes. Where's Thompson?"

"She's not with you?" Hesitant.

"No. I'll come out." Endland turned to Dent, nodded at the airlock controls. He slung the spear on his back.

Are you sure? Dent formed the words silently. He nodded.

The robots went out, too. She didn't try to stop them.

Outside, Endland asked again, "Where's Thompson?"

"Nowhere."

"Not headed back to Earth?"

"Not unless ghosts can travel without a ship."

"So why are you here? What do you want?"

"A battery," Devlin said. "Ours were... damaged. After you left."

"So take power off the ship. The fuel cells should last for months. Maybe years."

"Yeah . . . they're not working either."

"You mean you destroyed them, trying to keep Thompson from leaving."

"Potayto, pototto. Can I come in, at least?"

"No," Endland said.

"I'm running out of air. Not much water, either. I have to get power or I'll die."

"Really? That didn't cross your mind when you were starting a civil war back at the *Dare*? Why didn't you just let them go?"

"And leave us stranded, no supplies, no equipment?"

"Why not go back, then?"

"You know why. I'd rather rule in hell than serve in heaven." Devlin's voice was ragged now.

"Earth was hell. That's why we left."

"Are you going to help me or not?"

"Not," Endland said. "You made your choices. Live with them. Or die with them."

Devlin pulled the knife from his belt and slashed at Endland, who swung the spear, parrying Devlin's blow. Alice circled to Devlin's left, Nevermore to the right.

"Thompson was my friend," Endland said. "Captain Severin was a good man. There are still rules, even on Mars."

Gasping, Devlin staggered, swung the knife at Endland again. Devlin fell against the spear and ripped his suit on the way down. Struggled to get up. Alice bent, put both hands firmly on his back.

Endland kneeled, turned the head of the prostrate figure, looked into the staring eyes. Seconds passed.

"Ready to come in," he said, finally, rising.

"What about Devlin?" Dent asked.

"You want him in there?"

"No." No hesitation.

"I guess he can stay right here, then."

The Sun rose. Devlin was buried under a pile of rocks on the other side of the ridge. A quick, easy job for the four of them."

"What now?" Endland asked.

"We have a planet to explore," Dent said.

"The food won't hold out forever."

"So we raise as much as we can, let the plants recycle CO2."

"It gets pretty cold, winter nights on Mars," Endland said.

"Bundle up, hope the batteries and photoelectrics hold out."

"Then what? Die on Mars?"

"Or we fix your ship," Dent said. "Send it to find another star system. I hear Alpha Centauri's nice this time of year. Or Betelgeuse. Wherever. We'd never survive the trip, but there are two very smart robots here who might. Maybe someone out there will want to hear our story."

David Rogers' *poems, stories, and articles have appeared in various print and electronic publications, including Star*Line, The Comstock Review, Atlanta Review, Sky and Telescope, and Astronomy magazine. His latest work is Roots of the Dark Tower: The Long Quest and Many Lives of Roland, available from Amazon.*

More about David and his work can be found at Davidrogersbooks.wordpress.com

Wyldblood
Magazine

Subscriptions

Fantastic new science fiction
and fantasy delivered
every two months

Six issues:

£35 (print)
£15 (ebook)

www.wyldblood.com/magazine

Little Buddy

W.T. Paterson

The chill in the air settled against the fading blue sky as Porter lugged an ancient wooden storm panel around the side of the house. The cold sand shifted under his boots turning each step into an arthritic nightmare for his knees. It felt like the end of an era. The summer house that once teemed with life now sat empty and cold leaving only the rat-a-tat knocking of a pesky woodpecker that wreaked yearly havoc on the panels. Buddy, his son, had always helped with the end-of-season board-up, specifically shooing away the bird, but the boy had moved to the big city for a fancy hospital job and Porter was lucky if he got a phone call every other month. Minnie, his wife, took over their Massachusetts house after her therapist suggested a trial separation now that Buddy had grown. Minnie agreed before Porter could weigh in and all but exiled him to his family's seaside cottage in Maine for the winter. A quarter-century worth of marriage dissolved like a cruel magic trick. One moment things were fine, and the next the veil lifted to reveal the great absence of a used-to-be.

The wooden panel slid into the de-screened slot and hooked into place with rusted latches. Porter rested his sore shoulders and aching back and looked out across the empty beach. The calm ocean barely rippled, more lake than tidal beast roaring with surf. With the summer crowds gone, the small town barely stirred. A part of him believed that being holed up in the place for the winter would bring some clarity to the situation, that the isolation would do him good until the rat-a-tat started up again.

Porter wiped his brow and then slapped the boards. The thick panels shook, and the knocking ceased.

He stepped outside and around the house toward the bulkhead for the final panels, and that's when he saw it; the creature hiding near the cement foundation of his neighbor's place. A baby dinosaur, a dilophosaurus by the looks and no bigger than a housecat, watched with cautious curiosity. Its yellow skin with red-striped belly sniffed the air through a long, ridged snout. The creature gave Porter a weak warning growl to reveal a curved row of small, jagged teeth.

"Monsters," Porter said under his breath, and shook his head at the wealthy summer goers like the Hartwells who loved to buy exotic pets in the spring only to decide they didn't want them come fall. Instead of heading to proper shelters, they stuck the creatures outside to fend for themselves and left town without so much as a second thought. One year, animal control wrangled a Chupacabra after reports of missing cats piled up, and a few years later, the carcass of a tiger was found in the snowy dunes frozen and starved. Finding the small dinosaur was, unfortunately, par for the course.

Porter closed the rusty bulkhead and went inside even though he wasn't finished. He held his fingers under warm water to melt the stiffness in the joints and considered phoning the town. From the kitchen window, he watched the dinosaur sniff around and make chirping noises, neck craned and eyes large as the shadows of the houses stretched over the dunes and onto the empty beach.

The dark autumn sky swallowed the day. No one at the town hall had answered when he called, so Porter left a voicemail requesting that someone collect the dino. *Poor thing won't survive the cold,* he said. *It's their blood. They need the heat.* Porter wasn't sure how he knew this, but he knew it to be true. Leftover details from his childhood fascination with predators perhaps, or something pulled from Buddy's picture book filled with sharks and crocodiles and yetis and wolves.

That book was still upstairs, he was almost certain. They read it together every summer until Minnie complained that Buddy should turn his interests toward more sophisticated prose and came home with books about the anatomy, and physiology, and medicine. She tucked the book out of reach where it collected dust and rendered the sturdy pages fragile.

What an odd thing to remember at a time like this, Porter thought as he sat on the well-worn and sun-beaten couch. The muted television glowed with his favorite trivia show as static crackled across the screen. He waited for the phone to ring. He watched in quiet until the contestants shouted with glee as a big-money gamble paid off huge. They danced and twirled and pumped their hands up and down like they had just gotten married, like they had a few glasses of fine wine and a belly full of prime rib and sauntered to the dancefloor still believing the person they married was who they believed they were, that an office job wasn't built to turn a man inside out, that unconditional love could actually heal a person, that paying hand-over-fist for a future that benefited everyone but themselves was a noble path. "Dreamers," Porter said, and tried to will himself into a nap. That type of happiness made him uncomfortable. It was exhausting, a game for the young. It was why those trivia shows never cast anyone over thirty, because anyone older knew the that the

world was a limited path with nothing but forced naps that wouldn't come in a cold and empty house inside of a town that only lived for a single season.

When the evening news came on and the weather forecasted only cold days ahead, Porter went into the kitchen to scrounge up some dinner. In a cupboard was an unopened box of Rainb-O's cereal, buddy's favorite. He purchased a new box every year in the hopes that his son would visit and they could both share a bowl like the old days. He didn't want to open the box, just in case.

In the back of the freezer, he found two steaks so frozen and frostbitten that they could hammer a nail. He took one out and ran it under the faucet resigning to finish installing the panels in the morning. Over the hiss of the tap, he could faintly make out the lonely wail of the baby dinosaur somewhere outside.

"Poor thing," Porter said, and against his better judgement, filled an unused bamboo salad bowl with water and walked outside. At the base of the front steps, he put the bowl on the ground and whistled for the creature. The long, gravel driveway wound around sleepy dune grass, cut through overgrown lawn grass, and intersected with a paved road lined with tall pines. The neighboring houses stood like vacated caverns. Crickets pulsed in the chilly air like the slow breath of a sleeping giant. A moment later at the edge of the shadow, the dilophosaurus poked it's head out from a patch of cratered dunes and sniffed the air. Porter clicked his tongue and pointed at the water. The small creature took hesitant steps and growled a curious growl.

"Atta boy," Porter said, and watched the creature approach. "Don't get used to it, though. Done enough charity for this lifetime."

The idea turned him sour. Why did he always have to do things for the benefit of others? Why was it his responsibility to fix things? There was that time at the restaurant where Minnie had a little too much and started in.

"We should call and check on Buddy," she said.

"He's an adult, Min, he's fine," Porter said, feeling the night balance on the edge of Minnie's fragile mood.

"People can be adults and still drown in the bathtub, Porter," Minnie said, cupping the wine glass with such ferocity that it was a miracle the thing didn't shatter.

"Ok. We can go," Porter whispered, and put on his winter coat. He tossed an extra-large cash tip onto the table in an unspoken attempt to smooth things over with their server – a college girl with large eyes and full lips.

"He thinks money will buy you," Minnie said, stumbling through the slurred words as the server picked empty plates from the table. "But he's not your type, is he?"

The server went flush and smiled politely, and something about the reaction made Minnie go ice age. She didn't talk to him for the rest of the night.

In the morning, she knew she had done something, but couldn't remember what.

"Jog my memory," she pleaded, rubbing her head. "You're upset, and I can't change if I can't remember."

"Said some things is all," Porter mumbled, and twisted the gold wedding band around his finger to let the feeling go extinct.

A chill ran Porter's spine, so he turned suddenly to go back inside. It startled the dinosaur and the creature reared back on its small hind legs. A scaley umbrella-like mane shot out from the sides of its head. It rattled like a snake, an unmistakable warning.

"Oh please," Porter laughed. "Been married for nearly three decades. Know what that does to a man? Teeth don't scare me, pal."

He chuckled his way up the cold and creaking steps and closed the door inside. As he turned the porch light off, he watched through the glass as the small dinosaur retracted its mane, approached the bowl with curious eyes, and gulped down the water.

That salad bowl was a wedding gift, Porter thought. *What an odd thing to remember at a time like this.*

Just past sunrise, the rat-a-tat returned—a crude wooden alarm to usher in the rising coastal sun. Porter pulled the thinning comforter over his eyes and tried to ignore piercing rap, but the tapping pushed awake-ness through his eyelids like the slow drip of a hangover. His bones ached, the fossilized remains of a great used-to-be. Once a man so sturdy he could board up the home by himself breaking a sweat, he now struggled to sit upright in bed. All those years in an office behind a desk staring into sheets and memos and computer screens left little behind, and what remained had eroded into sun damaged skin and liver spots.

Rat-a-tat. Rat-a-tat. Rat-a-tat.

Porter slid out of bed still in jeans from the day before and shoved his wool-socked feet into tired work boots.

"I'm up," he grunted, and wiped the last bit of sleep from his eyes. He put on the same flannel as yesterday and walked downstairs. The bones of the quiet home creaked with every thumping step, the arthritic walls wailing and moaning too. With day old coffee sitting cold in the cloudy glass pot, Porter poured the thick mass into a mug and tossed it into the microwave. A single spotted banana stared at him from the fruit bowl and he considered the possibility, but instead watched the digital seconds count down until the ding produced a steaming cup of bitter jet-fuel. After one sip, he knew it had turned but he finished the mug as to not be wasteful before heading outside to finish the job.

A familiar dull pain pulled at the muscles between Porter's shoulders as he lugged another wooden panel from the bulkhead to the side of the house. Two more, and then he could shelter without worry of those winter storms.

Rat-a-tat. Rat-a-tat.

Porter shoved the panel into the sand below an open slot and huffed. He wanted to confront that damn bird, the constant pecking and relentless picking, but what good would that do anyone? No matter what he felt, the bird always came back and the rat-a-tat became a wooden, mocking laughter. At least with Buddy around, the boy could chase the bird through the cool and crunching dunes until he got tired, or bored, wanted to help with the panels. But Minnie always came outside demanding that Porter do something about the incessant, belligerent, ridiculous racket.

"It's fine, Minnie," Porter would say.

"Some people come here to relax. Some people need quiet reflection," she'd say, and flap back inside chirping about how she married the only man in the world who couldn't stand up to a bird. Buddy would watch from the dunes with large, confused eyes until Porter explained that it would have been Uncle Marius's birthday.

"Oh," the boy would say, and spend the rest of the afternoon quietly chasing birds, and bugs and while his father boarded.

Now, as Porter turned the corner of the boarded-up porch, he saw the small dinosaur crouched in the grass watching the gnawing woodpecker.

"Get!" Porter said and swiped at the bird. The dinosaur tilted its head. The woodpecker did a quick loop in the sky and swooped back onto the sill with an anarchic rat-a-tat. Porter's blood boiled and his ears went hot.

"I said…" he shouted, and the bird took off again. This time, as it swooped over the dunes, the young dilophosaurus expanded its scaley mane and spit a dark glob of venomous, paralyzing phlegm, which wrapped the bird and brought it crashing out of mid-air. The woodpecker landed lifelessly in the nearby sand. The baby creature trotted over and ate the remains with big, proud bites and then looked at Porter with glistening, hopeful eyes.

"Not bad, little buddy," he said, and though he couldn't be sure, it looked like the creature smiled at the compliment.

For the rest of the morning, the dinosaur walked along the sand and dunes chasing away seagulls, butterflies, and crickets that came too close as Porter fixed the final wooden panels into place.

At lunch, Porter cooked the other remaining steak, but something chewed at his wandering thoughts. The spotted banana eyed him from the fruit bowl, and Porter knew that sometimes cooking for one was really cooking for two. He slapped the steak onto a Corelle plate and popped outside. The dino poked its head out from between long blades of dune grass.

"Eat up, you done good today," he said, and balanced the plate on the bottom step of the stoop. The creature sniffed the air, eyed Porter, and scampered out to devour the cooked meat. Porter peeled the yellow banana back and ate the sweet fruit—though he didn't enjoy it—happy to be able to lend his talents to an appreciative crowd.

"If I let you in, you gonna be good?" Porter asked. The dinosaur looked up and continued chewing. "You gonna be good? If you come inside? You'll be a good boy?" The creature pondered the question like it understood, and finally chirped as it stepped toward Porter's knee. He gave it a gentle head-butt. Porter reached down and rubbed the top of the scaley head with his tired, heavy hands. "You're a good boy."

The baby dinosaur leaned back and sneezed. A tiny fleck of black, venomous phlegm landed on Porter's knuckle and burned the skin with a terribly, fiery pain.

"Sweet mother of mercy," he said, rubbing his fist on his jeans. The creature shrank with alarm when it realized what it had done, eyes wide with a different kind of hurt. "Ain't your fault, boy," Porter said. "It's just how you are." He stood to walk inside, and then whistled. The dilophosaurus perked up and followed, trotting next to Porter's knees but never crossing in front.

Porter started to suspect that something was different that evening. Not wrong, but different. The dinosaur took a wheezing nap against the electric baseboard heater of the thin-walled coastal home. Upon awaking, he watched Porter as though trying to communicate something.

"You hungry?" Porter asked, and the sound of his voice seemed to put the creature at ease. The young dinosaur rolled to his feet and tip-toed over to the couch and placed his scaley and unusually heavy chin on the top of Porter's thigh. Porter smiled and rubbed the creature's rough and uneven head. He noted the retracted mane on the neck like wrinkled skin and wondered at nature's design. The dilophosaurs relaxed into comfort, but the type of comfort that stems from concern and, he wasn't sure how, but Porter could sense it like a light left on in a room he was no longer using.

When he moved his leg, the creature stepped back and followed him into the kitchen where the man pan-fried a chicken breast and put it in a ceramic cereal bowl – the big one that Buddy always filled to the brim with colorful Rainb-O's but could never finish, until the year that Minnie insisted he switch over to something more nutritious like sausage and hash browns.

"A growing boy needs protein," she said. "You keep giving him this, he'll stay small forever, and be fragile, and his bones will be weak."

"Ok," Porter said like a deflating balloon, because every fight with Minnie was an unwinnable task. She fought with the fury and guilt over her wheelchair-bound brother Marius who drowned in the tub as a teen while she took a brief nap. What could he say to curb venom like that? Nothing, and Porter absorbed every last bit until there was nothing left.

The creature chomped at the chicken breast and pulled it apart with a ravenous hunger until everything was gone.

"You've got some appetite, lil' buddy," Porter said, and opened the cupboards to try and find something else to feed it. All that remained was the unopened box of Rainb-O's. He rattled the cardboard and the dinosaur tilted its head. Porter popped the top and poured into the ceramic bowl. The creature sniffed the sugary O's, looked at Porter, and then slowly lapped up the bits with his dark tongue. It only made it halfway through before walking away from the bowl, back into the living room, and pushed himself against the heater.

"How about a bedtime story before the sun goes down?" Porter asked, watching the young dino give in to heavy eyelids and long, strained breath. He knew just the book, it had to be here still.

Upstairs in the closet tucked in the very back of a shelf was the picture book of predators, the thick and sticky pages the same as they ever were. He remembered nights going through the pictures watching his son's wide-eyed wonder at sharks, and coyotes, and lycans, and felt the venomous sting of a used-to-be erode the sides of his heart.

Downstairs, he sat on the couch and whistled for the dinosaur. The creature lifted its head and walked with a sleepy limp over to Porter, who opened the picture book and read aloud the simple prose. With each picture he pointed to, the creature seemed to smile and drift further into the clutches of sleep, seemingly happy to hear the man's voice.

Porter's worry began to peak. The creature asleep at his feet sounded like it was having more trouble breathing, and it kept twitching with miniature seizures. He didn't know if this was natural, or a cause for alarm, so he pulled the phone from his pocket and wondered if his son might take a call in the big city. Wondering things such things made him feel insignificant, burdensome, left behind.

"Hey Pops!" a voice answered, which startled Porter. He hadn't been aware that he even dialed, and it sounded like his son was at a restaurant, or a bar, or out with friends being social.

"Hey Buddy, it's your father," Porter said.

"I know. Call ID. What's up?"

Porter wasn't sure where to start, or how to even ask. Stuttering through ideas, he blurted out the only thing that sounded plausible.

"What do you think about having a dinosaur as a pet?" he asked, and then held his breath for the reply.

"Nah, you don't want a dino. They have to have their own feeding space because they need to eat live meals. Birds, goats, sheep. Lot's of blood and entrails, pretty

heavy cleanup. Only raw food. Their micro-gut biomes are so strong that cooked food doesn't get transferred into nutrients and they'll starve to death. No people food. It makes 'em sick, like dogs and chocolate. A lot of work, too much work, Pops. Why? You, uh, you doing ok?"

"Oh yes, yes. Just daydreaming is all," Porter said. Dread rose from his chest into his throat as the creature kicked out again, writhing in some sort of pain. Porter did what he could to mask the anxiety. "How did you get so smart, anyways?"

"Years of mom forcing me to read books about how bodies work. Go figure," Buddy said. "Hey, can I call you back in the morning? The firm just got a grant and we're out celebrating."

"Of course, son. Sure thing," Porter said, and wheezed out a half-hearted, lonely laugh.

He hung up the phone and bent over the creature. The skin didn't feel right. He wasn't sure what *right* should have felt like, but this wasn't it. Dry, too dry, and far too warm in the head, while the yellow belly with red stripes felt too cool.

"Don't do this to me," Porter said. "Please, I'm doing the best I can."

The creature opened its eyes and chirped, but it was a distant noise. The pupils irised like a dimming bulb.

"I didn't know any better," Porter said, taking the head into his arms and cradling. "I did the best I could with what I knew, with what I had! I'll try harder, please!"

The dinosaur began to shake and froth. Porter couldn't look away even though the sight physically pained him, this creature in so much helpless, needless pain. Had the little dinosaur been like this all summer? Slowly starving to death?

A rattle began in the creature's chest, which forced the remaining air from its lungs like a tea kettle coming to boil. Porter physically felt the life inside the dinosaur diminish, and he broke down into tears.

"I could have done better, I wasn't ready for you, but I'm thankful we had this. Know that I'm thankful we had this," he said. A small spark of life came to the young dinosaur's eye and for that brief moment, they saw each other in the cold room. Porter wasn't sure how he knew, but he knew that dinosaur loved him in their short time together.

And then, as the sun dipped over the horizon, the remaining light turned to darkness, and Porter was alone.

Porter barely slept, if he even slept at all. After carrying the creature into the basement and deciding to bury it in the woods later, he couldn't shake the image of the dinosaur's last moments and how this all could have been prevented with a little attentiveness and research.

Rat-a-tat. Rat-a-tat. Rat-a-tat.

Porter wasn't in the mood. Of course another bird had come. Of course.

Then he realized it wasn't a knocking, but a ringing. His cell phone vibrated against the wooden night table with an incoming call from the town offices.

"Heyo, Porter, it's Len from City Hall. I didn't wake you, did I?"

"No," Porter said, and sat up.

"Anywho, got a call from the Hartwells asking if we'd seen a small dinosaur. Said it escaped as they were packing up last month. I told'em you'd called with a sighting, and they said they'd swing by. Wanted to give warning."

"Thanks Len," Porter said.

"Ayuh," Len said, and ended the call. The morning sun forced its way through the thin drapes with blinding reminders. It didn't seem fair that days got to start and end.

Porter sat up and put on his flannel, the same as the day before, and noticed a few places where venomous phlegm has burned small holes through the fabric. He ran his thumb over them and felt the immediate, pressing absence of a used-to-be.

Work-boots on, he limped downstairs with cold and tired knees as a shining car with New York plates blasting loud, electronic music pulled up the drive. He saw a young man and woman in their early twenties in the front seat, dark sunglasses pulled over their eyes, hair styled like they had just come from a fashion magazine's photo shoot.

"You the guy?" the woman asked as she stepped out of the car in high heels.

"Len said you'd seen our dinosaur. Tricky bugger snuck out while we loaded the car."

"Over those dunes," Porter said, pointing away from the house. "I was boarding up. Saw'em hiding near the beach."

"Is he still there?"

Porter shrugged and shoved his aching hands into his pockets. The woman rolled her eyes and whispered to the guy that she couldn't walk in the sand with heels, and that he should go, and that he better be quick because she wanted to get back to the city by nightfall.

"We have a buyer, you see," the guy said. "Top dollar."

Porter didn't move as the Hartwell boy traipsed into the dunes and whistled, pushing aside long blades of grass to look for any sign of the creature. He walked near the beach, deep into the grass, and then back again before returning to the car.

"Anything?" Porter asked.

"It's a baby, how far could it have gone?" the woman said, annoyed. She leaned against the car and scrolled through her phone.

"Maybe you should have kept a better eye on it," Porter said. He took his hands out of his pockets and crossed his arms.

"Excuse me?" the guy said and took off his sunglasses. He stepped into Porter's personal bubble.

"You left this town two months ago. Never once came back looking. You can't treat things that way, can't abandon something just 'cause you're bored. You have to love it. You have to try at least and sometimes stand up for yourself, even when it's hard, and you have to commit to working through tough times. Otherwise, anything that matters goes extinct and everyone ends up alone."

"It's just a dinosaur, dude," the guy said. He held up his hands like he was trying to ward off a charging bull.

"Let's just go," the woman said. "We'll tell Franco it was hit by a car or whatever."

The woman opened the passenger door and sat down as the guy stomped around to the driver's side cautiously eyeing Porter. At the end of the road, a familiar car turned into the drive. The car with New York plates turned around and sped out of the gravel drive as the other car—Buddy's car—pulled in. Buddy parked and stepped out into the slowly warming day. He stood with large shoulders, a yellow and red striped sweater hugging his frame. Though he hadn't been away in the city for too long, Porter couldn't believe how much his boy had grown.

"Hey Pops," Buddy said, holding an overnight bag. "What did those clowns want?"

"Something they shouldn't have," Porter said. "What's the occasion?"

Buddy shrugged.

"Talking to you last night, I dunno, thought you might enjoy some company."

Porter hugged his boy and welcomed him inside. With the wooden panels up along the porch wall, the inside felt cavernous and dark, but Buddy brought a certain light to the rooms that hadn't existed in quite some time. They chatted in the kitchen about life in the city, about Porter's move to the seasonal home, about the split with Minnie and how situations never stopped evolving.

"It's good to see you, though," Porter said after a while.

"No way, is that a box of Rainb-O's? Haven't had those in years. Don't tell mum, but…" Buddy said.

"Say no more," Porter said. He went into the cupboard and pulled out the recently-washed bamboo salad bowl.

"A growing boy needs his nutrition," Porter said. Buddy sat at the kitchen table like a happy child while Porter popped the top of the cardboard cereal box. He poured the colorful O's until the bowl had nearly filled and the box had all but emptied, and sat with his son in a warming house as daylight spilled through the cracks of the ancient wooden panels illuminating the presence of an always-will-be.

W. T. Paterson is a three-time Pushcart Prize nominee, holds an MFA in Fiction Writing from the University of New Hampshire, and is a graduate of Second City Chicago. His work has appeared in over 80 publications worldwide including The Saturday Evening Post, The Forge Literary Magazine, The Delhousie Review, Brilliant Flash Fiction, and Fresh Ink. A semi-finalist in the Aura Estra short story contest, his work has also received notable accolades from Lycan Valley, North 2 South Press, and Lumberloft. He spends most nights yelling for his cat to "Get down from there!"

Dust and Memories

Koji A Dae

A familiar scraping came from the nursery, followed by a low barrage of curses and then, "Diana!"

I groaned and looked over at Francie frozen in her walker, her head cocked to the side. "Daddy's moving furniture again."

"Diana, can you come here?" Justin's voice was louder, more insistent.

"Stay right there, baby." I tossed my book on the coffee table, ruffled her curly hair, and padded to the nursery.

The crib, changing table, and toy chest were islands in the middle of a sea of books, clothes, and toys, emptied into piles to make moving the furniture easier. Justin stood by the dresser, sweat dripping down his reddened neck.

"Again?" I gestured at the mess.

"It's spring," he said, as if the season explained his never-ending drive to reposition the furniture in our house. It's not that he practiced Feng Shui or believed in cosmic energy. That would be frustrating but bearable. He just couldn't leave well enough alone, like a child picking at an infected scab. "I need help with the dresser. It's not heavy, but I'm afraid it'll scuff if I drag it."

He pointed to the patch of parquet where the crib had been, now swept, mopped, and wiped down with polish. Some women would envy a man who cleans as fastidiously as Justin.

I pushed a loose hair from my ponytail behind my ear and grabbed one side as he lifted the other. We waddled to the opposite end of the room and Justin said, "I went my whole childhood in the same room with my furniture in the same position. And it's in the same position now.

There are dust bunnies the size of dinosaurs breeding under it."

Remembering his red eyes and scratchy throat every time we visited his parents, my heart melted with sympathy. "That's just because no one lives with your parents anymore so your mother doesn't sweep that room. It's possible to clean around the furniture just fine without moving it."

"It's always been like that. Speaking of, we should visit my mother soon," he said as I left the nursery. "Maybe this weekend."

While Justin finished rearranging, I packed a bag for us and Francie. We drove at night while Francie would sleep in her car seat. The moon danced between the curly hairs of Justin's trim beard. With every passing mile he spoke less, growing into a sullen man-child until his jaw clenched down and silenced him altogether. I didn't bother asking him what was wrong. He always turned cold when we went to his childhood home, and he never told me why. Prying just made him even more cranky.

We made it to my in-law's house slightly after midnight. Paula, wearing a cotton nightgown, greeted us in the driveway and whisked Francie out of the car while Saul, muttering under his breath, helped Justin grab the bags from the trunk. Upstairs, Francie woke and we ate a late supper. After nearly falling asleep in the soup, Paula took Francie and shooed us off to Justin's childhood room.

I sighed with exhaustion and started peeling my shirt from my travel-sore torso. But as Justin flicked on the lights, I let out a muffled scream. Saul sat in a worn armchair in the corner, staring off into space. He didn't flinch at my squeal of surprise, and his lips moved in a murmur too low for me to hear.

He grinned up at Justin with a faraway look in his eyes. "Justin! My boy. I'm glad you're here."

Justin and I shared a glance, somewhere between heartbreak and irritation, and Justin helped Saul back to the living room.

Alone, we settled in the fresh sheets of the double bed on the lower level of the bunk bed he had once shared with his brothers.

"Maybe we should bring Francie in here with us," he suggested, even though he was already half-naked and fully relaxed.

"You don't think your dad would do anything to her." I laughed at the thought of kind old Saul hurting a fly, let alone a child.

"Not on purpose, but he wanders more now. It's getting worse."

I kissed his cheek. "She'll be fine." I really meant his father would be fine, and I think he took the meaning, because he collected me in his arms and settled back to sleep.

Minutes later, as I drifted off, Justin let out a forceful sneeze. "Did you remember my allergy pills?"

He could spend hours dusting every nook and cranny in our house, but he couldn't pack his own medicine. "You can buy more tomorrow."

The wet scent of old books lining the longest wall infiltrated my nose as I slept. The dust from beneath the heavy cupboards stirred within the currents of our breath and came to my open mouth where it coated my tongue in tastes of the past and pushed its way down my throat to mix with my mucus.

Vibrant dreams drifted around me. At first just sparks of images, as if they were pieces of flint trying to catch fire. Eventually entire pictures took form. Clouds in a summer sky. I lay on my back as a child. Except the back didn't feel like mine. Neither did the clouds. A shiver ran through me and the scene shifted to snow falling in the winter. I pressed my nose to the bedroom window, and the cold made me laugh, sending a path of steam up the glass.

Justin tossed in his sleep, smacking me awake with the back of his hand. I groaned and pushed him back to his side of the bed, where he alternated between whimpers and groans until he settled again.

In the morning, a wheezing cough turned my voice to a croak. Apparently Justin wasn't the only one allergic to his parents' house. Paula's chatter floated from the kitchen as she offered Francie too many choices for breakfast. Water streamed through the old pipes, and I briefly entertained the idea of joining Justin in a hot shower. But grogginess pinned me to the bed. My head pounded with the footsteps of a hundred fleeing dream fairies, and my lungs gave a weak sound like a broken accordion.

A cough built in me. At first it came out as a light wisp of air, but my lungs got into the rhythm of it and spewed up a clot of mucus. Still refusing to get out of bed, I held the phlegm in my mouth. It was thick. Almost meaty. Fascination pushed disgust out of the way. I rolled the strange thickness over my tongue, then, with a moment of bravery, crushed it between my teeth. It popped like salmon caviar. I sat up to find a tissue, but as I righted myself, the room swam around me.

A sweet and astringent flavor filled my mouth. Cherry plums, like the ones Justin plucked from the trees whenever we went on walks. But instead of my usual disdain for the taste, I found a deep pleasure from the fierce battle being fought in my mouth. The dry, bitterness won. I smiled and spat out the pit. The bitterness always won. Cheap nylon backpack straps dug into my shoulders. The days were getting hotter, and the rest of the way home had hardly any trees. I reached up and grabbed a handful of the fruit before leaving the safety of the shade. On the corner, I spat a pit onto a small rectangle of grass—the last bit of grass before passing through the industrial zone. Knowledge that I had done the same thing, every day, for the past school year filled me with smug satisfaction.

I swallowed the loogie and the vision vanished around me. For a moment I had lived as a ten-year-old boy. I had felt the way the sun pleasured his skin and tasted with his taste buds. I made my way to the kitchen to drink a tall glass of water and wash the flavor of the vision from my mouth.

Paula offered to watch Francie while Justin and I went shopping. Picking up a few necessities for our apartment, without a child in the cart, counted as a luxurious date for us.

As we wound our way out of his neighborhood and through the industrial zone that separated his parents' house from the city I asked, "Is this the way you used to walk to school?"

He made a turn at a corner with a small patch of dry grass and a small cherry plum tree, showing off its first pinkish blooms of the season. "Sure, mostly. My brothers walked the long way around. They didn't like the guard dogs."

The tree was the one from my vision. It had to be. The one that was a seed in my mouth. No. Not mine. My husband's. It had grown strong and broad, like Justin had.

"You planted that tree, didn't you?"

"Huh?" He glanced where I pointed and a brief smile flitted over his lips. "Yeah, maybe, by accident. How'd you guess?"

My lips parted as the car swung into traffic and we left the corner behind. How could I explain to my husband the things I had seen that morning? He would brush it off as a coincidence. A dream. Perhaps he would be right. I might have been half

asleep, still in the magical place where pictures fill a person's mind. Knowing he ate cherry plums or walked this way wasn't exactly Earth shattering. A coincidence or, at most, a manifestation of my subconscious.

When we returned, Francie was playing with a ball in the yard near the chicken coup. Saul pulled weeds nearby. I offered a wave and we headed upstairs where Paula was cooking lunch.

"You left Francie alone with dad?" Justin clenched his jaw and I put my hand on his bicep to steady his anger.

"I had to get started on cooking. Besides, your dad's having a good day. They're fine. Francie's good for him." She continued chopping onions on a cutting board, not bothering to look up at Justin.

"She might be good for him, but what about her? She's just a toddler."

I flushed at his words. Saul was becoming more and more like a toddler. Soon he'd need to be reminded to use the toilet and Paula would have to help wipe him. Paula's chopping slowed.

"Justin, she's fine," I said. "You just saw them. The window's open, I'm sure your mom would hear..."

Paula wiped her hands on her apron. "I'm about finished here. I'll go check on them."

She turned off the empty pot on the stove as she left.

Justin plopped into a chair and dug a packet out of our shopping bags. He fumbled the package open and took out an allergy pill before passing it to me. The blister pack was light, the pills wrapped in a thin film of plastic and aluminum foil. I popped one out. They were tiny to contain such powerful relief.

"You should be more gentle with your parents. This is hard on them." My fingers closed around the pill but, instead of lifting it to my lips, I pushed it back into the blister pack. What if my vision hadn't been a coincidence or a dream? Another night of wheezing and coughing would be nothing compared to a deeper understanding of the childhood Justin rarely talked about.

"I know. I guess I didn't sleep well last night."

I put my hand over his and squeezed.

With someone else to listen for Francie's cries, bring her water, and comfort her through the night, Justin and I let ourselves indulge in a bit of touch. Our embrace quickly turned sweaty. Passionate. Seven years together and the need to become one hadn't eased. I pulled him close. Closer. Into me.

The physicality was enough. We both shuddered and groaned, appropriately low for the venue and appropriately urgent for the act. But at the final moment, when I wanted to collapse into him and disappear, the wall slammed up. He never felt it, or at least he denied it whenever I talked to him about it. But there it was—a sentry marching back and forth over his heart, refusing to let me into the innermost chamber.

"What are you hiding, my love?" I whispered as I wiped his sweaty hair from his temple. But he was already asleep.

I lay there, breathing the scent of stale childhood. He'd slept on this mattress. Or maybe the one above us. He'd read these books. He'd played with the toys scattered along the shelves. This wasn't his parents' room, even though it was in their house. It was a child's room. My husband. His two brothers. It was their island in the world.

A hacking fit broke me from my melodrama and, with a sip of water, I let myself join my husband in sleep.

Again the night was a confusion of sensations. Existence. Emotion. Joy. Tinges of pain. Fear—the kind that made dogs bark and hair stand on end. Beneath the emotions lurked scenes. Grain slipping through my fingers as I fed the chickens, trying to keep their scent off me as I was already in my school clothes. Building a model plane, painting blue stripes on the side, the smell of the paint filling the room with the hint of a garage and life as a mechanic.

I laughed at the thought of Justin in coveralls, his face smudged with grease.

A hand poked my ribs. "Diana!"

My eyes fluttered open. "Huh?"

"You were laughing in your sleep."

"Was I?" I smiled in the dark. "I had a funny dream."

I kissed his soft lips. His hand reached beneath my top. No mechanic's callouses. How far people drift from their childhood selves.

In the morning another coughing fit shook my body as I washed my face. I hacked in the bathroom until a thick secretion worked its way out of my lungs. Blood? No, just dark with dust particles. This time I held the phlegm in my mouth on purpose. Would it work again?

I bit down, gagging at the thick, rubbery texture as it squished between my teeth onto my tongue. No sooner did the ball break apart then I was transported out of the small bathroom to an open field. Sharp grass poked up at the sensitive skin on the back of my arms. It wasn't quite summer, but the days were long and slow. My eyes closed against the bright sky and a bittersweet emotion rushed through my chest.

My boy self didn't care to name the emotion. It was familiar to him. But I struggled to pin it down. It didn't have the longing of loneliness, nor the shriveling of guilt. Sorrow? Something along those lines.

Feet pounded against the path. Hushed voices carried dark laughter to my ears, and my dream self sat up. Dread washed across the blue sky. Two kids came by — older than I was. Bigger. Faster. Meaner. My brothers. They chanted taunts I couldn't hear. But I could feel the pelting of items on my skin. First the stinging kisses of green cherry plums and then the harder bruising of rocks.

My skin split where the missiles hit, and I ran. My feet weren't fast enough as they flew across the uneven field. The boys gained on me. But a secret filled me with hope. I ducked into a clump of bushes. Their thorny branches scratched my tender skin, but I pushed deeper, into a drainage pipe that stank of standing water. I pressed myself against the cool concrete and my breath slowed.

Kids said the pipe was haunted by the spirit of a rabid dog. Its depths rumbled like a growl, but I was pretty sure it was just the wind pressing through the tunnel. Either way, my brothers wouldn't follow me. But I wasn't sure how long they would lie in wait. I settled onto the dank ground and sat, listening. Minutes passed. An hour. Two. My body shook with a chill. I took on the stench of the enclosed space. The sky grew dark.

I spat and was back in the warm moisture of my in-law's bathroom. I splashed my face again but couldn't snap out of the fog that wrapped itself around me.

"Were your brothers mean to you?" I tried to sound casual as I buttered a piece of toast.

Justin's cutting glance let me know I failed. "Yeah, they were, you know, brothers."

I didn't know, though. I didn't have brothers and had only met his on a few rare occasions. They hadn't seemed close, but I'd assumed that was due to the age difference, not because they were sadistic brats. "Did they throw things at you? Torment you?"

"What are you getting at?" He picked up his phone, as if ending the conversation. But his question gave me an opening, and I jimmied into it.

"I had a dream. I saw your brothers throw those cherry plums at you." I didn't mention the rocks, even though they had stung more. "You ran away to a clump of trees and hid in a drainage pipe."

His finger stopped scrolling, but he kept his eyes on the screen. He didn't answer.

Maybe it was all in my mind. I sat next to him and bit into my toast as he turned on a news program for us to watch.

After Francie fell asleep for her nap, Justin jerked his head towards the door.

"Let's go for a walk," he mouthed.

Once outside, he relaxed his shoulders and stared at me as we strolled through the gate towards the field near his parents' home. His gaze warmed me more than the high spring sun.

"What's on your mind?" I took his hand.

"I want to show you something." His voice was low, almost nervous, as if we were first dating again.

He led me through the field. With the memories of my vision, I saw the yellowish grass through new eyes—the eyes of a child. Instead of a small patch of land between my in-law's house and the interstate, it became an immense place to get lost in. My heart fluttered as I set foot on it, and I wondered if Justin's heart pounded with the thickness of his memories.

We plowed across the field. When we rounded a corner, I gripped his hand so tightly he pulled away.

"That's it," I said. "That's the place you hid when your brothers chased you."

He pushed through the clump of bushes, even more overgrown than they had been in my vision, and found the mouth of the pipe, still just as dank and cold as it had been twenty years earlier. We had to stoop down to enter it. He had been so small. The smell made me gag, but I swallowed down my reaction and stood by Justin.

"Did they do it often?" I asked, resting my forehead against his chest.

He wrapped his arms around me. "Often enough. You know my brothers have another father. I don't know the details, but their childhood with him was difficult. I guess they thought I deserved a similar childhood."

He released me and led me from his little hideaway. In the fresh spring air, with the sun shining down, my shivering stopped.

"What I want to know is how you had this dream, so specific, when you didn't know about this place."

I bit my lip and chewed over the truth before deciding what to tell him. "It wasn't a dream. More of a vision." I explained my theory about the dust carrying his feelings into my dreams and collecting in my phlegm overnight. "In the morning, there's enough built up to inspire a real vision. I wasn't sure at first, but now…"

He wrinkled his nose. "That's disgusting."

"Absolutely."

"And you think it's from all the dust under the furniture?"

"What else could it be?" I shrugged. "Your house is filled with ghosts in the form of dust bunnies."

"I wondered why my dreams were always so vivid here. I thought it was just being back in my room." We returned to the field, and he tugged me down to the rough crabgrass.

"I think we should clean the room. Give it a good scrubbing. But first…"

He narrowed his usually wide green eyes. "First?"

"I want you to try it."

We had to stay an extra day for the allergy medicine to leave his system, but by the next night he was coughing and wheezing even harder than me. In the morning he hacked and gagged and gave a deep roar that turned my stomach. Phlegm is disgusting, but the loogie of a grown man will always outweigh the gentle snorting and coughing of a woman.

"Now?" he asked, his question slurred with the slime he held in his mouth.

I scooted back and turned my head. "Oh, god, ew, but yes. Now."

He chewed, his jaw working its way up and down with care. When his eyes took a distant stare over my shoulder, I knew it had worked.

It was mere seconds before he spat the material out into a cup. His breath came fast.

"So?"

His wild eyes told me the quality of his vision. "It works."

I touched his clammy face and his eyes danced around, refusing to meet mine. "What did you see?"

"I… not now. Let's just clean this room, okay?"

I pressed his head to my chest and gave his shoulders a squeeze.

"You know that whatever they did to you, you can tell me, right?" I whispered into his hair.

"Yeah. I know." He pressed away and looked me in the eyes. "Someday, I promise, I will. I know it's hard for you, when I don't talk about my past. Your patience has been amazing."

His forehead was clammy when I leaned forward to kiss it. I could spend a month in that house and roll around in his secrets. He wouldn't have to tell me anything. But instead of extending our stay, I went to the kitchen to ask Paula for a mop and bucket.

"Whatever for?" she asked, handing Francie a pickle.

"We want to clean out the back room. It's dusty."

She paused in her chopping and stared at me. "I'd rather you not."

"It's not a problem. Really. We're the only ones that use the room, so we can clean it."

She shook her head. "You don't understand. I don't want anything in the room changed. Saul likes to go there and remember his boys. He sits in the dark, and in those moments, I think he's happiest. I can't take that away from him. Not with everything else he's lost."

I wanted to say it's only dust, but I shut my mouth. I remembered Saul sitting in his chair, staring into space in a happy stupor. Happy or tragic, who was I to deny him his memories?

We drove at night again, neither of us talking about Justin's parents, the dust, or his brothers. The next morning, after walking Francie to daycare, I found Justin in the kitchen. A steaming cup of coffee sat in front of him as he stared out the window. I touched his shoulder, and he twitched, almost a jump.

"It was bad, wasn't it?"

He nodded. "I'm glad you didn't see it all. Just the surface dust. There are layers beneath that."

I fought the urge to ask for details. They would come, in time. "Do you want to rearrange our room?"

"Are you serious?" he asked, finally taking a sip of coffee.

"Yeah. I get it now. We can't let that stuff build up."

"That stuff, no." He focused on me, as if seeing me for the first time that morning, and a smile melted across his face. "But when I'm old and my mind is gone, I'd love to come back to my memories of you and Francie. And I swear, Francie will have a childhood she won't mind reliving when she visits."

Koji A. Dae is a queer American living in Bulgaria with she/they pronouns, a husband, two kids, and anxious depression. When not writing she enjoys dancing the blues and spending time in nature. You can find a full list of her writing at kojiadae.ink.

Plant Man

Leonora Lewis

Folks on the back roads of Florida, Georgia, Alabama, Mississippi, and Louisiana knew his dusty old beat up pickup truck that might have been white once. They called him the Plant Man. Mr. Arkady, owner of Arcadian Nursery and Plant Sanctuary. That's Arcadian, spelled A-R-C-A-D-I-A-N, not Acadian. I got to know him pretty good on account of the fact I worked for him back in the early seventies.

"Can your son come work for me? I have some jobs need doing."

I'd been lying on that old beat up sofa Mama kept on the front porch of the place we had in Ocala, Florida, smoking my last cigarette down to the butt when I heard someone talking southern with a foreign accent to my uncle.

"He's my nephew not my son." Uncle Bo said. "Ask him yourself, Plant Man."

Uncle Bo's wife, Mama's sister, had run off with my last stepdad, so Uncle Bo and Mama had taken to comforting each other. My uncle had a real *laissez faire* attitude toward me that made him a big improvement on Mama's past two husbands. He had only one hard and fast rule. "Boy, if you want beer or cigarettes, you gotta earn the money for them yourself." No fussing about me not being legal age.

The man came out the front door onto the sleeper porch and stood over me. Huck Finn all grown up I noted figuring I'd add that to my notebook. That's what I thought anyways, which would have surprised my teachers who didn't know I actually liked to read and kept a notebook. He wore a crumpled sweat stained broad brimmed hat he kept jammed down on his head.

Later, I found out he wore that hat all the time, never took it off even indoors.

"Tommy Maddox, you want a job?"

"Outdoor work?" Looking at the muscles on his arms underneath reddish hair and freckles, I already knew the answer.

On the other hand, if I wanted more money for beer and cigarettes, I couldn't be too choosy. Working outside beat flipping burgers and dealing with asshole customers.

"Hard work." He didn't beat around the bush. "You look like you have a strong enough back for it, but do you have the brains for it?"

"I guess we'll find out." I figured giving up the rest of my afternoon would be good for a little spending money.

"Now, Boy, we get the hell out of here." Mr. Arkady revved the engine and we drove back down the dirt road he'd turned off onto with the palm we'd dug up on that posted property in the back of his truck.

It was a lot more than the rest of my afternoon. We had driven miles following little two lane back roads through woods and swamps, long enough for me to get nervous about who I was with and where we were heading. We must have been getting close to the Florida-Alabama state line when Mr. Arkady turned onto a dirt road and parked in the ditch right by a big sign blaring "Future Site of the Crystal Creek Shopping Center" in big letters.

By the long shadows anybody likely to be coming or going on that road had already come and gone. We pulled up the barb wire enough to wriggle under the fence with the shovels without doing any damage to ourselves. Mr. Arkady led me a ways into the woods where we dug up the big palm he pointed out to me. Somehow we managed to roll it back to the fence, squeeze the palm and ourselves under the wire and lug it back to the truck.

Mr. Arkady had a tub and a sack of soil waiting in the truck bed along with a rope and a winch. "Now's the time for a little teamwork."

Each time I did something wrong with the ropes, I stopped to be yelled at, called "stupid" and told how to do it right, but Mr. Arkady never said a word. He'd indicate I needed to pull a little more here or brace myself and we kept going until we had the palm planted in the tub and drove off.

"We stole a fucking tree."

Mr. Arkady turned to look at me. "The site was going to be bull dozed. It's a Queen Sago palm. People pay hundreds of dollars for them."

From that first day of plant poaching, Mr. Arkady had me hooked. I made it out of bed and showed up at Arcadian Nursery and Plant Sanctuary first thing the next morning. I didn't see Mr. Arkady around so I rambled up and down the aisles. I was peering through the pots of orange flowered azaleas when I locked eyes with a girl. A real pretty girl with brown hair and the dark eyes of a doe. She startled just as easy too, running off on bare feet, her dress more like a nighty flapping around her.

"Hey, miss?"

I took off after her. Skidding around a corner, I ran right into Mr. Arkady.

"You got another job for me?" I asked trying to look over his shoulder to see where the girl disappeared to.

That's how a way to earn a little money turned into a permanent part time job. I became a pretty good collector, keeping my eyes peeled for plants that sell for good money growing in the woods or on the side of the road. I'd figured out the more stock

Mr. Arkady got for free the more Mr. Arkady could afford my paycheck.

Besides that, those girls kept turning up among the plants when I worked around the nursery mixing up the peat with sand or repotting the plants that had outgrown their containers. I'd see them out of the corner of my eye. The one I'd first seen and a couple of her friends; a blonde though I swear her hair looked light green, and a tall straight girl with silvery ash hair.

The three of them would be peeping at me from behind a display, pointing and giggling. As soon as they realized I'd spotted them, they'd take off. All of them moved like the girls in my school who took ballet.

Not a whole lot different from school where the girls would look at me, giggle, and take off. I'd look after them, figure I couldn't catch one of them anyway, and get back to what I'd been doing.

Sometimes on our out of state collecting trips, like the one where we dug up some bug-eating pitcher plants in Georgia, I'd start to ask Mr. Arkady about the girls. But I always held back.

"You want to say something, boy? Spit it out." He'd say.

"Nope. Not important." I had a good thing going and didn't want to mess it up.

Mr. Arkady taught me old house sites were good places to collect roses and camellias. I'd spend a whole Saturday collecting orchids. The real expensive ones grew on oak trees. Mr. Arkady kept a special section of the nursery just for them.

We didn't always sneak around. Some of the contractors got to know the Plant Man and let him know where they would work next so he could get in ahead of them. Now and then some real unusual characters came in out of nowhere. Like that old fellow I had pegged for a Seminole.

Turns out he was a Mississippi Choctaw who'd come to tell Mr. Arkady about a white spiderwort. That sure got

Mr. Arkady all excited and off we went heading for Mississippi in that truck.

"Oh, and by the way, Plant Man, could you take a look at my sheep while you're at it? They're not doing too well."

While Mr. Arkady was checking out the sheep, I waited in the shade. The old Choctaw looked at me.

"You know Plant Man's an Old One. Not one of ours. He came over with the white people. You know that? Right?"

I just shrugged. I didn't know what the old guy was talking about.

I was actually in school when Principal Langley caught me and hauled my ass out of class.

"You weren't in school yesterday."

I hadn't been in some last week either. In fact I missed quite a few days every month. "Yup."

"You better have a good explanation."

"I was at my job."

"You have a job?"

"Yes sir, I do."

"Uh-huh." Principal Langley looked over his glasses at me. "Where've you been working lately?"

That's when I explained about how a plant someone buys for twelve to fifteen dollars in the nursery costs twenty five to fifty or more when they're delivered and planted. Delivering azaleas to new sprung up subdivisions means good money. I'd leave at seven in the morning. Mr. Arkady'd hand me twenty dollars for lunch and send me out with the truck loaded with deliveries. I'd drive a big circuit making it back at seven in the evening. Twelve deliveries, twelve fat packets of money.

I reeled off some of the fancy names builders put up on bill boards. I'd been in and out of most of them.

"That's off Old Church Road?"

"No sir, That's out in that new Sandy Pines subdivision."

"Reckon you've been planting palms out there."

"No. Azaleas do best. Mr. Arkady sort of talks people into going with what grows best and will stay alive. He says it's not good for business to have a bunch of yards full of dying plants that come from him."

"Seems like Mr. Arkady still has all his marbles. Enough to notice if any money goes missing or too much of his gas gets used up." Principal Langley looked at me like he'd never really seen me before. "Tell you what. I'm going to declare you work-study. We'll adjust your hours out per week. I'll never bother you again."

It wasn't only about money. The Plant Man loved everything we collected. He'd walk around the misting tables where the small plants grew in orange juice cans we knocked the bottoms out of. He'd talk to them in a foreign language or play those strange reed pipes of his low like wind and bird song. He kept a special walled locked garden for his favorites and rare plants. University professors came to him about those, including the famous LSU professor who put us up in his house on the iris collecting trip.

We'd been collecting irises from bogs in Louisiana when we came upon him. A fellow in wading boots and hat bent over a tripod taking pictures of an iris, adjusting the lens with a blue veined hand. The old fellow takes his flower picture before straightening up and looking us up and down, then he relaxes, pulling his hat off his thinning hair, his face splitting into a grin. "Plant Man. I always figured we'd have to meet up again sometimes."

The professor put us up in his house, one of those nice ones on the Baton Rouge City Park Lakes, and tagged along with us talking with Mr. Arkady like they'd been friends forever. I helped the prof haul his cameras and tripods around while he'd set them up and take pictures of the irises and other wildflowers for the book he ended up writing before we'd collect some of them. The prof's the man, who when he accidentally saw some of my scribbles talked me into submitting them to a college magazine and dang... if they didn't actually publish them.

I discovered Mr. Arkady played a mean harmonica. I heard him when he met up with some musician on the way back from Louisiana. Anyway, Mr. Arkady and I were heading back through Saint Tammany Parish when this old man walking by the side of the road holding a guitar case flagged us down. Musicians, they traveled around and let Mr. Arkady know where they'd seen surveys marked, then we'd go in collecting wild plants just ahead of the bulldozers.

Mr. Arkady got out of the truck and they started talking. Next thing I knew he handed me the keys. "Take the truck and find a place to spend the night. Pick me up here at this spot next morning."

So, I decided to look up Stevie Mouton, who I'd gone to school with from kindergarten until Momma married her second husband and took us off to Florida.

"Guess the Grunches didn't get you after all," Those were Stevie's first words to me. We'd heard about Grunches, half sheep half man who wandered back roads looking for people to eat, from some kids from New Orleans back at a church camp.

Steve and I stood out in the front yard catching up when his mom comes out the door all dolled up. "She's heading to the honky tonk. She does this when Dad's out on the rigs in the gulf." Steve says loud enough for her to overhear.

I don't judge. My own Momma and Uncle Bo were heading for a breakup. Just a matter of time. I thought about Uncle Bo away for weeks at a time driving the tugs that pulled barges down the Mississippi. So of course, Steve's mother walked over and slapped him upside the head before getting in her car and driving off. Didn't stop Steve from laughing.

"Come with me. I'll take you to a place with some of the best music you ever heard, but we've got to walk. They don't let you in if you drive."

Steve leads me through the woods that came out to this old ramshackle place off a dirt road, an old building covered in tar paper, probably an old smoke house. Inside Steve pulls up a trap door and we go down the rickety stairs into this big room full of people dancing and drinking. The place is dim but there are lights giving out a soft glow and I realize they've lit the place with jars of fireflies.

"Hey, man, aren't you worried your momma will show up here and see you?"

"Naw," Steve answered. "Not her kind of scene."

There on a platform in the middle of the room in the band jamming away stood that old fellow from the side of the road with his guitar, a drummer, a fiddler, and Mr. Arkady blowing away on the harmonica. He looked up, saw me, nodded and kept on playing.

Someone placed a couple of jelly jars full of the goldenest beer you ever saw in front of Steve and me. Like drinking liquid sunshine. Someone, I forget who, told me they made it from fermented honey.

Steve and I stumbled back through the woods in the dark, both of us in a real good mood from the music. When we came out on the dirt road, there was a parked car, jouncing up and down fit to break the axles, windows all fogged up.

Steve said, "Told you my momma was going to the honky tonk."

On my day off I went tubing on the river. I was just lying back listening to bird song looking at the clouds and tree-tops passing by letting the current carry me wherever. Next thing I heard the music, low and breathy, coming from behind the old big willow hiding a little branch off the main river.

"Mr. Arkady?" He must be out collecting. I spun the tube around and paddled beneath the curtain of willow leaves, keeping an eye out for any snakes hanging down.

Clearing the willow, I looked up and saw big water birds, Great Blue Herons, that's what they looked like anyway, wading in the shallows among the lily pads, others roosting on overhanging tree branches.

Mr. Arkady walked along the bank, his pants rolled up to his knees, bare headed for the first time ever, almost skipping playing his pipes. A couple of the big birds bobbed up and down on their long skinny legs around him. Every now and then he'd lay his ear against a tree trunk listening for something.

He leaned against a southern sweet bay with its large flat waxy leaves and large creamy perfumey flowers which don't stink like a southern magnolia. Before I started working for him I couldn't have told a sweet bay from a southern magnolia. I did good to tell oak, sweetgum, and pine from one other but not much more than that.

He seemed pleased with that tree. That's when I saw his hairy leg propped up on a cypress root ended in a hoof. He had little, not so big you'd notice right away, horns on top of his head.

"Traack! Traack!" Right then one of birds dancing around him spotted me and started squawking and flapping its wings.

The others began to cry. "Chirou! Chirou!"

He looked right at me, opened his mouth and began to scream like nothing I ever heard before. I clapped my hands over my ears and pushed away with my feet spinning the tube around and around in a blind panic getting the hell out of there. Only later I remembered the two birds on the bank ran around scratching out his tracks in the sand.

Plant Man's caught up with me on my family's sleeper porch, only there's no family. I got home and found Momma gone, the house padlocked, and my stuff piled up on the porch. I had gone back to my rust bucket wheels to get a wrench to break a window. That letter from Uncle Bo saying how to reach him and he'd put in a word for me on the barges had to be somewhere inside.

I had taken a swing with the wrench when my arm was caught in a powerful grip. I hadn't even heard Mr. Arkady come up behind me. He must have parked his truck up the road.

"I'm not the Devil, Satan, Lucifer, Beelzebub or Old Scratch if that's what you're afraid of. Now you know I've got a special job for you. It don't look to me like you've got anything else to do."

He's got his pants rolled down and workman's boots on his feet covering his hooves, his pipes sticking out of his shirt pocket along with a pen and index cards; his broad brimmed hat shaded his head from the sun hiding the two little horns I'd seen sticking up out of curly reddish brown hair streaked with gray.

"What happens to me next time we're out back of beyond, you being a Grunch and all?" I blurted out.

"Don't you know your sheep from goats, boy? New Orleans folks are full of bullshit. If you want to know what I am, back in ancient Greece men called me Pan."

"One of those old Greek gods?" I guess I knew deep down inside he wasn't the devil, but it made me feel better to have a name for what he was. Then I remembered some of the old stories of what happened to people gods thought spied on them.

He pulled his hat off giving me another look at his curly horns growing out of his head of curly hair. "You're afraid I'm mad on account of you seeing. That I'm worried about you telling. Like the ancient king with donkey's ears. The only man who knew was his barber and the secret got to be too much for him. It don't matter to me what you tell. I've been around this long. Are you quitting? Yes or no?"

He told me he figured out long ago he wasn't really a god, had probably never been one, while he helped load my stuff into the truck. He considered that day a great liberation for him.

"We'll set up a cot in an empty storage room when we get back." Mr. Arkady said.

We went and collected the southern sweet bay I'd seen him noting on the river bank. No small job. We had to go in and out with a john boat, and then put it in a tub of good soil before hauling it off in the truck.

Once we got it unloaded, he told me to pull the pallet into his special personal garden, the one he kept locked, all the way to the grove he'd planted of his special trees. He had a couple of oaks, a sweetgum, a tulip tree, a couple of poplars and a black cherry. "I want you to see something."

What happened then? Mr. Arkady pulled out his pipes and began to play. At first I thought it was the breeze that made the branches move. Then I saw all the leaves on the other trees were rustling in time to the music. A girl stepped out from behind the black cherry. The one I'd seen behind the orange azaleas. A couple of more showed up stepping out from behind trees.

Arkady started skipping and whirling in and out among them." Bring some beer." He called to me.

Next morning I woke up on the grass in the arms of the first girl I'd seen. She smiled, said something in a foreign language that sounded like pigeons cooing, blew me a kiss, walked into a tree and disappeared.

"Dryads." Mr. Arkady stood there leaning against another tree. "They live in trees. I find them and bring them here to keep them safe from all the building and tearing down that's going on. I don't know how many have been lost to clear cutting."

I guess you could say that Mr. Arkady led me astray, plant poaching, hanging out in backwoods blues clubs, losing my virginity with a dryad. But he also led me into gainful employment. The day I graduated he called me in and showed me a letter.

"Time to move on." Mr. Arkady had sent the LSU Professor, the one who wrote the book on southern wildflowers, my SAT scores.

I stared at the letter saying I'd been accepted to LSU.

"You can't keep on doing what you're doing for the rest of your life. You're smart, boy, though you do your best to hide it."

He was right about that and other things. A secret like the one about Mr. Arkady being Pan, that's too big to keep, so I wrote a book. I put in everything I'd learned about the woods and swamps, about the Choctaw and the Seminole, about Pan and dryads and called it fiction.

It sold pretty well. In fact I'm on my way to a book signing now. I still keep my eyes open for the Plant Man driving his beat up old truck on the back roads of Florida, Georgia, Alabama, Mississippi and Louisiana. Maybe I'll run into him one day when I'm out rambling the woods where sunlight and shadows play along a creek bed keeping company with long legged water birds. I'm sure one day I'll hear the sounds of his pipe calling in the deep south summer breeze.

Leonora Lewis lives in Texas in a house full of books, plays violin badly, and is an active member of the Woodlands Writing Guild. Her work has appeared in Bubble-Off Plumb, Timeless Tales Magazine, and the 2020 WWG Anthology Insight.

Interview with Sole Refugee from the A303 Incident

James Rowland

For the purpose of record-keeping, Anna, can you please give your full name, address and occupation as it was before the incident?

Uh, sure. Anna Cottrell, 12 Lincrest Street, Sevenoaks. I work as a tax specialist.

Excellent. And why were you on the A303 at the time of the incident?

Well, we'd just been on holiday. I was feeling bad that I hadn't spent enough time with the kids, so we went to Cornwall for half-term week. Just the three of us. And –

Can you tell us a little about your children? Names, ages, that sort of thing.

Oh. Yeah. Umm, Holly is my eldest. She's 17 and doing well in sixth form. A prefect and everything. And, Michael is 15 and about to start his GCSEs. He's a good kid. A bit of a troublemaker, you know, but he's got a brain on him. He's a right little artist too.

And the father?

Divorced.

I'm sorry I had to ask. We just need to get a clear record. You're the first direct contact we've had with someone who was on the road at the time. If we're going to understand exactly what happened, we

need to make sure there aren't any gaps. So, you were on holiday in Cornwall?

Yes. We had a great time. Beaches, pasties, fudge. Everything really. The plan was to leave on Tuesday of the next week, so as to miss the traffic. Oh, the schools would have been annoyed, but I would have just written in a note saying the kids were sick. And I'd get to spend another couple of days with my babies. But something came up at work. You know, always another big meeting. This one was on Friday and I really needed the week, so we left early Sunday and hoped to avoid the rush.

And you didn't?

We were hardly passed Exeter before the traffic began. It wasn't too bad at first. Still moving, anyway. But 60 miles per hour became 40 and then 20. I thought about trying to get off the main road, maybe head along the coast past Weymouth, but it just seemed too much effort. I figured there had been a crash and everything would clear up soon.

But it didn't?

Obviously.

So where did you come to a standstill?

We hadn't been on the A303 for long. Probably south of Buckland St Mary.

And the car didn't move again afterwards? Everything else you did on foot?

Yeah. It was total gridlock, you wouldn't have been able to get more than a bike moving.

Okay. Now, Anna. We really need to understand every aspect of what

happened in these early hours. We're absolutely blind as to what happened here, and to be frank, that's not good. So, please, tell us what you remember after you came to a stop.

There's not much to say. I mean, you don't think to leave your car at first. We just sat there, everyone did. I kept the car running for a time just for the air conditioning, but Mikey suggested that might kill the battery, so we just sat there with the windows open. Everyone else had the same idea. It all got a bit annoying. It was like being on a train. You know, so many snatches of conversations and songs, but they all drowned out the other, so you really didn't hear anything.

The children were fine. Mikey noticed that we had no service, but he just played games while Holly read. They know how to distract themselves, always have since I'm often busy. I was worried about getting home late. I wanted to be well rested for the work week. But it wasn't too bad. We had some fudge in the car, so we just snacked while waiting.

And when did people first start to leave their cars?

After a couple of hours, I suppose. It happened like a Mexican wave. I could see people climbing out of their cars way in front of us, and then a little closer, then all around us, and finally people behind were stretching their legs too. I think nearly everyone was out by the afternoon.

You included?

Eventually, yes. Holly and Mikey were keen to have a walk about, but I didn't want to be out of the car in case the traffic started to move.

But everyone else was out of their cars, so how was the traffic going to move?

That's what Holly said. I got out then. I was just worried about the meeting, I guess.

So, what happened once you left the car?

Well, we sort of wandered. Not too far, just stretching. Mikey can talk the ear off anyone. He might as well be an old man from up north, so he went off and chatted away. Holly and I stayed together. No one went off the road straight away, which was good, and soon enough a few parties broke out.

Parties?

Most of the cars were filled with people on holiday, like us. So, everyone had coolers and camping chairs. Families sat around eating and drinking whatever they had in their cars, and others joined in. Soon, the road was filled with these little parties. Seemed like every direction I turned, I could hear a hundred different songs. The road smelt like a picnic. Honestly, the wind tasted like salt and vinegar crisps. Mikey and Holly went off to where some teenagers were working their way through some fizz. They even played volleyball using an old Mini as a net! It was nice to see them making friends so easy.

I somehow got dragged into a cosy, little group near my car. All parents, chatting away about their trips. There was a guy there that said something had happened in Basingstoke. He had a few drinks, so I think he was just bullshitting. Telling a tall tale to impress some of the single mums. But he said it was something big. Like a radiation leak or something. One of the other guys said Basingstoke didn't even have a nuclear plant. Do you know what happened?

How long did you stay with your car?

Oh, a couple of days. It sounds stupid whatever way you think about it. Why would you leave your car on the road and walk? It's just a traffic jam. But then, what traffic jam goes on for days? We argued about it for a bit, but I was starting to worry about my work meeting, and eventually I thought we better start walking. We locked the car up and just hoped that no one would loot it. People were behaving themselves anyway.

There was no violence or looting at all?

No. Like, people argued. People always argue, you know. But it never got really bad. We all just buckled down and dealt with the situation. It was great, almost. It's like we were proving that humans weren't always a total mess.

I imagine the food and drink people had disappeared quickly, though?

Definitely. No one was rationing anything. Why would we? We expected to be on the move again in no time at all.

So, the supply drops came as a huge relief then?

They were lifesavers.

Tell me more about them.

Why? You sent them.

It was certainly made to look that way, wasn't it?

Well, from the first morning after gridlock, drones appeared above. Funny little things, really. Smooth and round, they buzzed about, always glinting in the sunlight. They flew back and forth down the road, dropping care packages. Water bottles and pouches. Energy bars. Trail mix. Fruit, once in a while. It wasn't exactly Masterchef, but it did the job. We weren't hungry. Once people started grouping together, the supplies became more sophisticated as well.

What?

We figured you were watching from the drones. Weren't you? After a couple of days, communities started to build. Just clumps of cars and so on, people who have made friends. And the care packages started to include pasta, meat, vege, all sorts, really. Even portable stoves so we could cook. People started to make communal meals. Big, hearty stews. You could smell it all down the road. The wind smelt like spices, beef and chicken. The water kept coming, but there would be fizz and alcohol too. People felt relaxed. Any frustration about the traffic sort of slipped away. Like the memory of an old book.

You moved on, though, didn't you? Why? Most people stayed with their cars, right?

Well, yes. The meeting was preying on my mind. But not a lot of people moved, I'll confess. The occasional person migrated. Often forward, toward the front of the traffic, but some people walked back as well.

To get out of the jam?

I don't think so. More… they were looking for something, you know? A group to fit into. A better fit than where they had been.

Did you ever witness anyone try and leave the road?

Most people saw someone walk. At least, after a couple of days.

And what happened to those people?

If you're asking me that, I think you already know. I don't want to explain.

I would like to hear an eyewitness account. It's the only way we can really understand this.

It's a strange place, really. You know, the West Country's like a different time. No cities or anything. Where we were, trees towered over one side and rolling, green fields on the other. It was like you might disappear into an older world.

People didn't disappear into an older world, though, did they?

No. They didn't.

Anna, please. What happened to them?

I only saw it happen twice. It was the same, both times. Men, too. I never heard of a woman trying to leave. I don't know what that says. Are men more decisive? Are we more in aware of our surroundings? The guys must have decided they had enough. They clambered over the hedgerow and began to walk across the field. It was as simple as that. They just walked away. We watched them, hearts in our mouths. Even the first guy, when we didn't know that something would happen. We just felt it. People say we don't have a sixth sense, but I really think we do. Intuition. Everyone watching that first man stepping off the road knew something was going to happen.

He, well, he started to flicker. Like he was walking into television static. Right in front of our eyes, he was fading from view. He noticed it too. He stopped. He stared down at his hands. He panicked; he began to scream. It... it didn't sound right. The scream was crackling. We should have heard him clearly, like a real person, but he sounded like a character screaming on a dying video. No one went to help him. What could we do? So, we sat there and watched.

A light emerged from the pit of his stomach. It grew and sizzled, burning away at his transparent body. It wasn't... it wasn't like watching a man die. You remember the old film negatives? We were watching a man-sized one catch fire in front of us, and when it was gone, there was only the suggestion of a memory of a man: footsteps frozen into the grass where he disappeared.

The other guy went like that as well.

And you never saw them again? There was never a suggestion of someone coming back?

No. They... they were gone.

So, most people didn't leave the road after that?

Not exactly. You didn't vanish if you stepped off the road. It only happened to you if you tried to leave the road. You needed intent. It was like a law being enforced. You needed to mean to break it. So, people who pulled out tents onto the grass, but never tried to walk away didn't get hurt. It was like the road was extending its territory out into the fields surrounding it.

Uh, right. So, people started to camp out by their cars, formed communities and survived on the care packages. But you and your family began to walk?

I had the meeting. I mean, England isn't a large country. I figured we could walk past the jam and call my mother to pick us up once we got phone service again.

Anna. Your children aren't here with us, are they? What happened to them?

I... well, I, it's, it was their choice. I guess there comes a time where you can't force your children to follow you. Maybe they never should? I wondered about that after they left. You wonder if you've given them all the life skills they need to survive. I hope I had, but... but, I don't know.

Anna. What happened?

Mikey left first, of course. He's old for his years. We'd been walking for a couple of days. Maybe ten miles each time? I don't really know. The cars just stretched on and on. It seemed like this was the only thing left in the world: this road, these cars, reaching out to the edge of existence. And everyone was really coming together. It was beautiful in a way. There should have been violence, rioting, stealing, but none of that really happened. Maybe, that was the point? A test?

At the end of one day, we stayed with a group of caravans. They had parked up on the grass, so the road could be a social space. At first, the kids used it as a football pitch. Mikey had the time of his life, another opportunity to let off some steam. I was exhausted, though. I gladly took up the offer of a camp chair and spent the rest of the evening dozing. Once the football game finished, they threw on some music and it became a dance floor while dinner was handed out. Some stew thing, I think.

He wanted to stay then. He'd made friends and enjoyed the communal feel. He even helped with the dishes! But he was my boy. I wasn't just leaving him behind. We had a terrible row. Caused a right scene. But the next morning, he was with Holly and I as we carried on down the road. He was quiet, though. We all were. There was less colour on this bit of the carriageway. The rainbow of battered cars seemed to turn into a monochrome, German train, and people stayed tight to their cars. It was dreary. The dreary middle class, never taking a moment to relax. I guess I should have been there, really. That was where I belonged? Mikey made it worse, too. He was a teenager, so he sulked. Kicked his feet. Slowed to a stroll. I could've slapped him. I didn't, obviously. I don't believe in that.

The monotony of the road was only broken during the evening. We came across, well, I don't really know how to describe it. A carnival? A commune? Someone told me later that this band had been on tour. Steels drums, mostly. They unloaded their van and had been playing most days since. Others joined in, and by the time we got there, it was like an artistic retreat. People painting. Singing. Writing. I don't know how they got the paint. A supply drop someone suggested. Why would you waste time dropping in paint?

I don't know. But please, go on.

I didn't stand a chance, did I? We set up camp that night and Mikey was gone in the blink of an eye. He played the drums. One guy said he had a knack for them. He talked to a pretty girl and she drew his face. He got hold of some of the paint and spent hours at the canvas. He was sold, and this time I knew I couldn't force him. He's fifteen. I couldn't just drag him down the road.

So, you left your son with strangers?

Don't say it like that. I had my meeting to get to. I knew he would be safe, and it wasn't like this was forever. I told him he should come with me, but when he refused, I said I'd come back and collect him when the traffic was cleared. He seemed pleased with that. He kissed me on the cheek and told me I should stay too. But I couldn't, you know? I had my meeting.

And what happened to Holly?

She's too good a person. Always has been. Heart the size of a giant. She wanted to help. Maybe, she needed to. She couldn't look away.

What do you mean?

The closer we got to the end of the road, the more people were… hurt.

Hurt?

Maybe. I don't know. It was like, uh, people were sleepwalking. They seemed okay, healthy, but they were obviously sick. They'd walk for a while and then collapse, crying, screaming. A doctor who was on hand said it was more mental than physical. There was nothing wrong with them. Everything was in their head.

These people came from the cause of the traffic jam?

Mostly. Some were just people who had been near the front. It wasn't uniform. Not everyone got sick. And those who didn't looked after those who did.

And Holly stayed and helped?

Yes.

And you didn't?

Don't look at me like that. How could I help? I'm not a doctor or anything. And I had my meeting to get to.

You were okay leaving your child behind?

No. I told her to come with me, to not be silly.

And what did she say?

I… It doesn't matter.

Anna, it really does. We need a full account.

She said… she said that we should stay. That it was the only thing we could do. She said we had missed my meeting. Why she would say that? Kept going on about how we'd been walking for a week, that the meeting was over, but that couldn't have been right. I still had time to make it. I had to make it. So, I told her to do what she wanted and I carried on.

How long had you been walking?

I… I don't know. A few days. It couldn't have been a couple of weeks. You must know, right? How long has it been?

That's not relevant right now, okay. You had nearly made it to the front of the traffic jam. Your children were safe behind you. What was it like near the incident?

The cars were more tightly packed, like proper gridlock. They were tucked in bumper to bumper. No one had move them to make way for communal living spaces. Not that there was anyone really living. Everyone had moved back down the line by then. I remember being annoyed. How was the traffic going to clear if no one was by their cars? The only people left were the few remaining sleepwalkers that hadn't been collected by people wanting to help. They weren't bothered by me, though. Left me to walk through the cars on my own, to reach the end of the road.

The end of the road? What do you mean end?

Oh.

Anna, please. What was waiting for you?

I'd forgotten about it. How did I forget? All that walking, and I forgot about the end of the road. How silly of me.

Anna. What did you see?

It was such a strange scene. Like a meteor had struck. The road vanished into a crater. All the green grass, the tall trees, they all disappeared. It was like England had been replaced. I stood at the tip of a great bowl, filled with chaos. Metal pulled into new, twisted shape. The afterthoughts of cars scattered across the reddish-brown earth. There were more sleepwalkers there. They rambled across the open space, occasionally bumping into each other. They… they were hurting, though. Blood. Screams. It was awful. Oh God, it was so awful.

Anna. Anna. It's okay. You're safe now. You're safe. But you need to tell us, what happened?

I… I walked on.

Into the crater? With all the bodies? Why?

The… the meeting. I had… I had to get to the meeting.

Okay. And what did you see? How did you get out? No one else has, Anna. You're the only person to step out of that crater. How did you do it?

I, uh. I don't remember.

Ann-

No, I don't remember! I can see it. I can see the crater from the outside, from the lip. I can see all those people. All hurting. Like the broken cars. I can see it. But… but I don't remember. I don't remember going in.

Anna, pleas-

I don't remember! I walked into the crater. And, and, and that's it. The next thing I know I'm here. I don't remember. I really don't. You have to believe me! Why don't I remember? Oh God, what about my babies? You have to get them. We have to get them! And the meeting. My meeting!

Okay, okay. Anna, please calm down. Anna. Anna, please. Doctor, Doctor! Anna. Anna, you're safe. Calm her down, please. You're free to run your tests. Just – just keep her alive. We'll want to question her further.

Please. Please, can you let me go. I really need to make my meeting!

You've been away for seven months, Anna. There's no meeting.

*Born and bred in Britain, **James Rowland** now lives in New Zealand where he works as an IP lawyer. He has a degree in law and history, both of which having a passing usefulness in fiction writing. His work has recently appeared in Compelling Science Fiction, Aurealis, NewMyths, and B Cubed Press's Alternative Apocalypse. He appeared on Tangent Online's Recommended Reading List of 2018 and 2019 and was shortlisted for Best Novelette and Best Short Story in the Sir Julius Vogel Awards in 2019 and 2020.*

No One Goes Lonely

J. L. Royce

"Wake up, sleepyhead! It's time for HappyKaf!"

The familiar jingle jolted Fred out of a bad-weather dream. He closed his eyes again.

The Happy Krew would be dancing around his futon, their raceless, genderless, *café au lait* faces singing merrily, and he just couldn't stand it. He was about to blink left to dismiss the ad, then remembered that too-real moment: coming, coming…*now*.

The aroma of coffee—*real* coffee—wafted through his augment.

"HappyKaf, your caffeinated breakfast beverage. Try HappyKaf Plus, now with antibodies! Enjoy your HappyKaf ad-free if you purchase in the next sixty seconds!"

The ad drifted away, since others were clamoring for Fred's attention.

A stentorian voice: *"Why's a studly cishet like you waking up alone?"*

A variety of women's faces drifted by, their expressions ranging from friendly to carnivorous.

"Update your profile today, and—"

Fred caught up with the departing coffee cup icon, blinked left, and bought the HappyKaf. The ads scurried away, and he sank into the rapturous quiet. With any luck, the drone would be delayed.

The blissful, ad-free silence ended when he finished the Kaf.

Fred was staring down at the stacks of dirty dishes waiting to be hand-washed in the vanity (his room being too small for a kitchen). The plates and sink suddenly disappeared, replaced by the vertiginous view from the crest of a waterfall: a hundred feet of cascading blue, plummeting into a bright, churning pool. The bathroom smelled of mist.

"Come on, Freddie!" The woman shouted from somewhere in the closet behind him. She ran past, all tan legs and bouncing breasts in a trikini, to leap off the precipice, shrieking. Assuming a graceful swan dive, she pierced the surface of the pool below.

Upbeat music followed.

"What are you waiting for" asked the Voice of Matchless. *"Take the plunge, with Matchless! If you update your profile in the next hour, we will pay for your ad-free day. If you hook up in the next week, you'll—"*

Fred sped through the spiel, then let the ad resume. Far below, the girl emerged from the churning water—her mask and top lost—and cried out, *"Jump, Freddie!— the water's great!"*

The voice-over concluded, *"Matchless—where no one goes lonely!"*

The waterfall faded, and Fred loosened his hands from the edge of the counter. In his augment, the Matchless *Update Profile* icon floated, challenging him. New ads began swarming like flies, jostling about his tiny apartment, vying for attention: hair removal, hair replacement; male enhancement, porn—on and on.

"Damnit!" Fred muttered, and blinked on *Update Profile*. The pending ads fluttered away, and the Matchless dashboard unfolded. The strong rhythm of the Matchless theme lurked somewhere around him…coming from the bedroom, of course. Fred knew the music would swell if he tried to ignore the app.

He stared at the ribbon of uploaded media scrolling along the bottom, his pathetic virtual outdoor shots and vclub scenes, clearly solitary selfies. Fred deleted the collection.

The profile text appeared in the mirror over the vanity. Fred studied it, the familiar cloying phrases. He hovered his gaze over the *Edit* icon, then chose *Delete* instead. The insipid self-description vanished, and the

Record icon appeared. Fred cleared his throat and chose *Voice Only*.

"My name is Fred. I enjoy moonlit walks on the beach—by myself, the only sound being the breakers and my own breathing. I enjoy cooking for one, when I can afford real ingredients, and reading by myself more than group-watching the crap that passes for entertainment in the mix.

"I live alone, and I want to keep it that way. I don't mind sex, but if you think it's the price you have to pay so we can talk, then I'm not interested."

Fred paused and took a breath, feeling energized. He resumed.

"I'm not being mean; I just want some peace and quiet—*peace* and *quiet,* So I'm refreshing Matchless to earn a day's respite from my augment adpay. If like me you're endlessly paying off an implant, then let's 'hook up', leave each other alone, and spend *thirty days* without ads. I look forward to blinking you in. Ciao."

Fred blinked on *Save*. The theme music swelled; the girl last seen bobbing in his vanity appeared and awarded him with a coy smile and a wink.

"See you later, Freddie."

The music wrapped up, and Fred prepared to enjoy washing his sink full of dishes in silence.

A salesperson wearing a knockout avatar had convinced Fred, in his senior year, that the road to financial success lay in becoming a mix influencer, live-streaming his augment. By the time his following had grown to a few thousand (the lovely avatar had assured him) the blink-throughs would more than pay for his augment and surgery, and he'd be free of the always-on adpay that was the price of his enhancement.

Free. That was the theory.

The reality was that Fred couldn't make it as a streamer, and could barely keep up on the interest payments, much less knock down the principal on the augment financing. So he was looking at twenty-three more years of adpay, sixteen hours a day.

Fred pondered his fate as he enjoyed the last hours of freedom. With adpay disabled, he could disengage his augment completely. He'd slept in—no Happy Kaf or YogaGoGo or MorningGlory wake-up calls—after a quiet evening of reading a book in silence.

The faucet dripped. There was a jittery whine in the HVAC that echoed through the ducts and drifted like a spectral presence through the room. Fred listened to these and other sounds, like the intermittent rumble of the express elevators rocketing up a hundred floors at a leap, and marveled at the real world that surrounded him, usually overwritten by the mix.

The refrigerator smelled. Not necessarily bad; just moist and animate, unlike the dry, scrubbed air of the apartment. After scraping together leftovers for breakfast (while humming the Happy Kaf jingle to himself), he masked up and went for a walk, determined to explore this world further.

Cars made noises, all on their own. The mix would normally supply cartoon motor effects or animal sounds or aggressive game-themed musical soundtracks. But in reality vehicles hummed and whirred like insects, the older ones sounding variously distressed or dangerous.

Masks concealed all the faces; without facial projections, there were no cheerful, optimized expressions. Some people mumbled as they walked, talking in their augments—conversations with apps, or avatars, or perhaps even real people. Others simply walked in an abstracted state of mix overload.

The air was full of smells—natural smells, no longer suppressed and replaced by the olfactory processor of his augment. Foods, machinery, people: all left an impression on Fred as he made his way down to the riverfront.

The usual clutter of pop-up virtual kiosks and targeted billboards in the mix was gone. It was amusing to watch the connected passers-by step around what Fred saw as voids. (For a while, he purposely walked through them. His augment soon warned that it would override and restore the mix if he persisted in such 'asocial ambulation'.)

Fred wandered down the Riverwalk, enjoying the unadorned stone path he hadn't noticed since his augment surgery: physical, free of signage. The twenty-foot tall anime personalities and corporate mascots that usually strode the broad walkway in the mix were absent. It was boring—until you noticed the patterns of shadows cast by the fencing, the ripples of sunlight on the river.

Fred splurged on a Happy Kaf from a wandering delivery cart, and lingered by the shore. The river had a natural aroma, of vegetation and fish both living and dead. He was leaning on the railing, peering into the water rolling by and sipping his beverage when his phone chimed: a message from Matchless.

Hi Fred—Would you like to see your match?

He paced the Riverwalk, sure it must be a mistake, or harassment. No one would read that profile and think he *wanted* to hook up. After minutes of indecision, he stopped and focused on the message to open the match.

She had a pleasant albeit serious face. If there were effects applied, they were minimal. There was a text.

Tanya: Meet F2F will explain.

Fred blinked on *Location* and was shocked to find that she was only a few meters away. Whirling around, he splashed Kaf on himself and switched hands, shaking the brew from his sleeve. He searched his surroundings, wondering why his augment wasn't identifying the pedestrians walking by, then remembered that it was off.

She was leaning on the same rail, just downstream, in unassuming sweats: real clothes. When they made eye contact over their protective masks she face-palmed, concealing her amusement at his predicament.

Fred walked over, still waggling his damp arm. "Tanya?"

"In the flesh." With effects off, he could only see her eyes—which made the encounter all the more intriguing.

"Hi Fred. Or Freddie? Matchless wasn't—"

"Fred."

They nodded in greeting, and flicked wrists to exchange contacts. Fred's augment chimed: still disabled.

"You bounced my card!" Tanya chuckled. "No foul. Isn't it pleasant, being alone? Peaceful."

Fred blinked his augment back on for basic comm. "Again…please?"

This time they flicked wrists a little more intentionally, he noticed, and her profile appeared.

"Yeah, it's a change. Shame it will end in—" he blinked on his clock "—thirty-three minutes."

"Good idea, though," Tanya said. "So you've been offline? Didn't check out my profile then, did you?"

"No—why?" He immediately brought up Matchless, listening.

"Hi—I'm Tanya. Here's a riddle that will tell you something about me. What's the difference between you and my dildo? Give up? The dildo talks less and performs—"

"Don't!" Tanya wailed in feigned embarrassment.

"It's funny!" Fred replied. "You're a funny person. Uh, sense of humor, I mean."

The breeze swept brown tendrils across her face. Tanya absently swept aside the fine hair, pivoting back and forth, one leg bent.

"It doesn't have to end today." She waited for a reaction.

"What do you mean?"

"The Matchless offer."

"It's only good for one profile update." Fred knew what she was alluding to, but wanted *her* to propose it.

"Not that." Tanya's eyes narrowed. "The expanded offer."

"Thirty days, ad-free," he said, "'…to spend with your new significant other'."

The proposal was tempting. Fred thought of the books he could read—he might even get some writing done.

"We'd have to declare a Match."

"Sure." Tanya shrugged. "What's so hard?"

She stopped her agitated wobbling. "Or is it that difficult to imagine spending a month near me?"

"Near you?"

She rolled her eyes. "Ever read the Terms? You know they'll track locations."

Tanya and Fred both glanced away, searching the *Terms of Use* in the Matchless app. She found it first.

"'…average distance between partners less than one meter for one-half of each of six days per week'," she recited, in a sing-song voice, "or the ads come back automatically."

Fred took a sudden interest in the river. Tanya filled the silence.

"You left your reading list in your profile. That's what caught my attention. Where did you *find* those books?"

"Mostly scans on the gray market, a few in actual paper. Online estate sales, mostly." He frowned. "I like paper. It's so hard to enjoy reading with a jingle every five minutes."

"Yeah," she agreed. "I read too. Public library online, mostly, but hanging out there means *PSA, PSA, PSA*—"

Fred laughed. She had a way of expressing herself that no mask could hide.

"You could share your books with me…" she suggested.

"Sit and read?"

"Or…whatever."

Fred mulled it. "We can't sit out in public for that long—the civil servitors will hassle us for violating public health rules."

"My place?" he suggested, immediately ashamed of his tentative tone.

"Well, I've got roommates," Tanya said. "Fem dorm, fellow inmates. Practically live in the mix-soaps. So…yes. Please. Your place."

"I guess you'd want to set down, ah, rules—"

"Like we don't have enough rules already? Why?" she asked. "Should I be worried?"

Tanya pivoted away from the river to face him, waiting for a reply. But Fred was staring at her chest—actually, the faded lettering on her worn sweatshirt.

"Hello?" she said, glaring. "Up here?"

"Elvish?" Fred knew; but did she? It was important.

He searched her face. Tanya looked tense. Fred was certain she was about to jump him: embrace him—or throw him on the ground.

"Meaning…" Tanya waited, eyes pleading.

"'One Ring to rule them all'," he pronounced.

"End of discussion!" It wasn't a passionate assault; Tanya bounced once in her running shoes, unruly brunette waves tossed into the wind. "When can we start?"

Fred realized he was in a decent negotiating position, and might as well admit to everything.

"I like to read lying down, since my one chair is broken."

"That's nice," she replied. "I like to read in my robe—with my dog in my lap. Mastiff."

"The dirty dishes pile up in the vanity until there aren't any left clean. I brush my teeth over them. And my building doesn't allow pets," he lied.

"Kidding!" she grinned. "I don't have a dog. And I don't own a robe either, so…"

Fred blinked his augment into life, focusing on Matchless among the icons gathering to assault him. Around the couple, the virtual stands and anime monstrosities appeared, clamoring for his attention.

Tanya brought up her hand, placed her wrist close to his. They looked at each other and blinked to link.

The jingle; and then, *Matched!*

Then: silence, and the faint smell of fish.

"Selfie together?" Tanya suggested. "Make it official."

He stepped closer. She smelled slightly of a pleasant hand sanitizer, and he made a mental note to refill his bottle.

"Sure. Turn on effects?" Fred stared into those eyes.

"Naw." Her eyes crinkled over the mask. "Just like this."

J. L. Royce is a published author of science fiction, the macabre, and whatever else strikes him. He lives in the northern reaches of the American Midwest. His work appears in Allegory, Ghostlight, parABnormal, Sci Phi, Stupefying Stories, Utopia, etc. Some of his anthologized stories may be found on Amazon: amazon.com/author/jlroyce.

They Don't Make Them Like They Used To

M.C. St John

Halley checked her schedule app and said, "One more stop and we are done for the day. How you holding up?"

"Fine," Oscar said. "The company knows I like the long routes. But I'm amazed you've put up with the routes *and* me."

Halley grinned. "How else am I going to prove my worth to Alpha? Turn here."

"*Claro.*" He steered the service van into a graceful arc, the electric motor humming. "Check me out. The AI vans got nothing on me."

Oscar was always making dad jokes. His sense of humor was dumb, but it still tickled Halley. She liked job shadowing him because of it.

Oscar was a spry, compact man with a clean-shaven face. He had a full head of dark hair that was turning salt and pepper at the temples. At certain times of day — usually in line with his energy levels at work — he could look anywhere between forty-five and seventy. But inside, he was perpetually corny. Some people, Halley had learned, were built that way.

"One day you'll be as good a driver as me," Oscar said. "I've seen your work. You got a real knack for the job. It's not all OS updates, like the company teaches nowadays."

Halley groaned. "I've sat through those trainings. Nothing but watching video clips and pressing buttons."

"Service calls are the way to learn our trade. You gotta be ready with your wits and muscles. I ever tell you what the *guitarrista* said to his mother before his automated solo?"

"Three times, I think."

"I'll tell you again. *Look, Mama, no hands.*"

"Every time you tell it, it gets a little worse," she said, "but I get what you're saying. The automated stuff doesn't beat real handiwork."

"If more apprentices understood that, they would have gotten my seal of approval."

"How are my chances?"

"Slim if you don't start laughing at my jokes."

"I'm always up for a challenge."

"You're going to get one," Oscar said. "Here's out next stop."

She flicked through the nav chart. "310 Isotope Lane. How'd you know?"

"Because the family's out on the lawn," he said, parking the van. "Let's put that handiwork of yours to the test."

They got out and made their way up the pristine sidewalk. Both of them wore company-issued coveralls with their service rankings based on the visible color spectrum. Oscar's coveralls were a rich violet that was slightly faded at the elbows and knees. Halley's were a fresh ochre, having graduated from the lower frequencies of basic training. She carried a chrome toolbox with the Alpha Company's logo, a line drawing of a gear with the infinity symbol at its center.

The short walk on Isotope Lane was picturesque. It was a pleasant sector of the Division, away from the older parts of the City. This Division neighborhood was designed in the mid-twentieth century American architectural motif. Lining each side of the street were quiet, repetitive homes painted in shades of mint, eggshell, and apple.

Halley and Oscar arrived at the drowsy, summertime hour before dinner, no doubt being grilled on the backyard barbecue and served with cool glasses of lemonade. Crickets chirped in the rose bushes. A soft breeze set wind chimes tinkling. Somewhere, the crack of a wooden bat hitting a line drive heralded the gentle good cheer of a baseball game crowd. For this small hamlet, all was well and right in the world.

The neighborhood council here, like others Halley had done service work for, voted to maintain June-level peacefulness all year round. Such financial efforts amounted to a suburban utopia, with precise climate control and streaming environmental ambiance. Anything to keep things pleasant inside their hermetically-sealed enclave was well worth the price.

Which made the sight of the family outside of 310 all the more distressing. They stood in a nuclear family tableau on the front lawn, caught in a scene of frozen panic: Wife gripping Husband, both staring hopelessly past Young Daughter to the far edge of the yard. They all watched the lawn sprinkler there, a retro model that sprayed a fine-laced fan of water. The scattered mist caught rainbows from the afternoon light.

It also outlined a silhouette.

"Do you see the boy?" Oscar asked.

They watched as the silhouette flickered. Pixels of detail grew and swirled. Now hanging in the air was a glass replica of a child, frozen in his leap through the sprinkler. More pixels swirled inside, bits of information filling in until—

Blip.

A boy in blue shorts appeared, as real as any of the family on the lawn. To Halley, the tableau now resembled adverts she had seen in the Division archives, images from

the very era the neighbors in this sector strived for: a picture of perfect suburban bliss.

But as soon as the boy had grown solid, he flickered again and vanished.

Blip.

"He's on the fritz," Oscar said. "These newer models are not waterproof, no matter how many times Alpha claims it. All right, service faces. I'll do the talking. You do the fixing."

Oscar flashed a smile to the family, who were now within earshot.

"Afternoon, folks," he said. "We see you have an issue with your son."

The wife broke away from her husband. She was a thin woman in a tailored dress. Wet mascara daubed the corners of her eyes. "Calvin was fine last week at the lake, but today...oh, it's awful seeing him disappear..."

"There's no need to get upset again," the husband said. His face was set in well-worn lines of concern. He turned to Oscar.

"I appreciate you coming out so quickly. Calvin was—*is*—a lively child, but we've made sure to properly maintain him."

Oscar nodded. "I've reviewed your file, and you're within your two-year service warranty. We're here to help, free of charge."

"I'm glad to hear it."

Marion let out a shaky sigh and spoke to Halley. "We try to take care of our Calvin. He had done so well with this upgrade. He glitched once or twice, but Tom never saw it happen. I convinced myself I was seeing things. You know how mothers can be." She turned to her daughter. "Greta, honey, don't get too close while the service people are working."

Unfazed by her mother's words, Greta continued to run around in her pink swimsuit. She circled the sprinkler, singing to herself.

"Calvin Shmalvin, he's off line. When will he reboot this time? In an hour, in a day? When will he come back to play?"

"Cute song," Halley said.

"Greta is his younger sister by two years," Marion said. "It's strange to tell you that, isn't it? He's not getting any older, unless we pay for a new OS. And she's growing up so fast. Soon enough, Greta is going to be the older sister, and Calvin will be..."

Halley laid a hand on Marion's shoulder. "The most important thing right now is getting Calvin back online."

"You're right, yes. And you can do it."

"That's right," Halley said. "I'll do whatever it takes."

"Wonderful. Just wonderful." Marion drew herself up, smiling. She wiped away her wet mascara. "Would you like anything to eat? Perhaps a slice of cherry pie? I had one cooling in the kitchen before...this. My oven 3-D printed it."

"I could go for a drink," Halley said. "Do you have real tea leaves?"

"My, what a request."

"If it's a bother..."

"Not at all," Marion said. "I do believe we have a tea tin in our fallout shelter. I can get a cup brewing. Any preference?"

"Any is fine. The longer it's steeped the better, thank you."

When Marion was gone, Halley turned back to the sprinkler. The boy Calvin was in his mid-leap again, at the precise moment where he was a real boy, or as close as Alpha could get to real. Then, *blip*—empty space.

At this angle, she noticed that the space was not entirely empty. Hovering there was Calvin's Alpha gear. It was the exact shape as the Alpha logo on Halley's toolbox, about the width of the palm of her hand.

Oscar joined her. "Good move with giving the mother something to do," he said. "The last thing you need is hearing her cry every time he glitches." He whistled under his breath, assessing the scene. "Okay, here's your test. What's the proposed fix?"

"The gear is in the pocket of his swim trunks. I can grab it with my work gloves and then manually reboot him. What? You're looking at me funny."

"*Nada*. The move is tricky, is all. What if the boy goes online before you finish?"

"As we both know, two pieces of matter have a hard time being in the same place at the same time. If my hand is where Calvin is supposed to be when he goes online, then I would probably lose my hand. If that happened, say goodbye to a service promotion." Halley tipped her head. "Come on, Oscar. That would be a rookie move, and a rookie I ain't."

"I'm making sure you know the risks."

"Does she, though? Does she really?"

Tom the father came over. He planted himself in between Halley and Oscar, his hands on the hips. He didn't look happy with either of them, especially Oscar.

"The Alpha vid rep assured me the service person they'd sent out would be highly qualified. I hear you talking to this young woman as if *she* will be the one repairing my boy. I see the color of her uniform. It's on the wrong end of the spectrum, frankly."

"She's a shade of yellow in service rank, not ability," Oscar said.

"I was under the impression from Alpha that your colors determined technical worth. That makes them one in the same, doesn't it?"

"Not to me," Halley said. "I take my work very seriously, and I happen to be good at it—frankly. We only want to help as best we can."

Tom regarded her, the lines in his frown deepening. "Marion and I invested all of our credit into buying Calvin's gear. I don't regret a single day of it, because he is back, just as Alpha promised. *A lifetime guaranteed*—that's your slogan. But we could barely afford this latest upgrade. A new model is out of the question. This gear must be repaired. So, understand my dissatisfaction with the phrase *as best we can*. It simply isn't good enough."

"Then allow me to rephrase. I *will* fix Calvin. So, let's start with step one. Can we have the sprinkler turned off?"

"The control panel is around back," Tom said. He glared at Oscar. "I hope your trainee knows what she's doing." Then he disappeared behind the house.

"*Aye*, me too." Oscar turned to Halley. "Did you forget the service etiquette rules? Alpha guarantees product and customer satisfaction to the ninety-ninth percentile. *Not* one hundred. What you said was reckless."

"Only if I fail. And I won't."

"There's a chance."

"Are you doubting me too?"

"I'm only reminding you about this concept called margin of error."

"I like your dad jokes, Oscar. Not your dad sarcasm."

While Halley assessed what she may need from the toolbox, the water shut off. Now a ghostly silhouette of Calvin hung dripping in midair.

Greta, who had kept singing and dancing, seemed to wake up from what she was doing and notice the two strange service people for the first time. She skipped over to Halley. "Are you gonna fix my dumb brother?"

"Do you see these? I'm wearing them so I can reboot your brother."

"Ooo, the colors are so pretty."

Halley examined her work gloves. The filaments lining the metal material were fine veins of phosphorescent light. As part of her training, she had to name every sub-class of optic fiber and carbon strand that made up these gloves, had to demonstrate the fine-motor techniques while wearing them to rewire, repair, and reconstitute any current Alpha product. But Greta's comment had Halley seeing the gloves anew.

"You're right," she said. "They are pretty."

Greta held out her hands and balanced on one foot. "I made up a song about Calvin. Do you want to hear it?"

"Oh, I heard it earlier. It's catchy."

"I like to make up things. I'm good at it." She hopped to the other foot. "Like how you're good at making up Calvin."

"We used everything your mom and dad gave us to make him. All of his genes and memories. He's your brother, through and through."

Greta considered this. "Last week, when we all went to the lake, Calvin jumped in the water and stayed under for a really long time. My mom got scared. She *freaked*. Because my dumb brother did that before. He jumped right in and never came back up. I was little, but I remember. I had a swimsuit with a cool unicorn on it."

"I like the mermaid on this one," Halley said.

"Mermaids are cooler than unicorns now. But Calvin didn't remember my old swimsuit. He didn't remember that scary time at the lake at all. So, last week, he went and jumped in again like before and freaked everyone out."

"He doesn't have those memories from before. We built him with everything else up until that point. Who would want to remember something so scary?"

"Not me."

"Me neither. But sometimes, Alpha people will repeat things without knowing it. We all can do silly things like that, can't we?"

Greta shook her head. "I do everything good."

"Everyone else does silly things. Eventually, though, we come out better on the other side. Look at your brother. He came out of the lake this time."

"When Calvin did, my mom almost passed out. He thought he was a real *cut-up*, like my dad says."

"I bet."

"Then Calvin tried to grab my ankle to throw me in, but I was too fast. He smacked himself good on the dock from trying. Look at how quick I can hop, see?"

"Super quick," Halley said, smiling. "Should I go fix Calvin now?"

"I *guess*. He's so dumb that a sprinkler messed him up. I told him last night his gear was cracked, but he wouldn't listen to me. I'm just widdle biddle Greta, and I'm a know-it-all. Well, I know more than *him*."

"Do you remember where you saw the crack?"

"Uh-huh. On the number eight, in one of the loops." Inspired by her own words, Greta did a twirl and ran singing across the lawn. "Calvin, Shmalvin he can't hear, when he broke his Alpha gear..."

"The *niña* is a chatterbox," Oscar said, "but she got that sass from her father."

Halley nodded. "She was helpful too. I know what's wrong with the boy."

"Yeah, what was that about the number eight?"

"She was talking about the lemniscate," Halley said. "The infinity symbol on Calvin's gear. It must have cracked when he was horseplaying with her." She tapped the back of her right gloves; lights in the fingertips turned a rosy pink. "I'll heat-seal it, and then reboot him."

"Remember to time it, because —"

"Yes, yes. *Look Ma, no hands.* I know."

Halley made her way to the sprinkler, her boots squelching in the wet grass. Down the street was the calliope jingle of an ice cream truck and the laughter of children following it. Real or manufactured, the sounds came from a world away.

Halley was focused on timing Calvin's glitching. It took fifteen seconds for him to go to a fully-formed boy, *blip*. He stayed that way for another five seconds. Then, *blip*—the Alpha gear hovered alone. She had about ten seconds of free time to handle the gear. She cranked up the heat-sealing temperature of her glove and got ready.

Now she was close enough to note the details Alpha had engineered. A constellation of freckles scattered across Calvin's cheeks. His strawberry blonde hair, still wet from the sprinkler, lifted in sheafs from his forehead and around his ears in mid-flight. Four of his baby teeth were missing; Halley could count the gaps in his wild, smiling mouth. Those details and a million others added up to Calvin. This close, the boy appeared as real as Halley herself. The Alpha Company lived up to its slogan: a lifetime guaranteed.

The boy started to flicker.

Halley held her breath.

Blip. The boy vanished again.

Halley reached for the floating gear. It was hot to the touch, thrumming hard from the glitch cycle it was stuck in. She brought the gear closer to her, flipping it over.

There: a knick in the casing, right inside the engraved infinity sign.

Part of the 3-D projector chip was exposed, but nothing more. If there was any water in there, it would evaporate as soon as she started heat-sealing. She placed the glowing thumb pad of her right glove over the knick. Sulphur and burning metal filled the air.

"Halley," Oscar said. "You have to hurry."

"I'm fine."

"No, you're not. Calvin's coming back. Don't you see him?"

She did. Within the heat-seal smoke, pixels appeared and swirled around. The boy was filling back in.

"He's about to *blip* back on," Oscar said, his voice rising. "You have to let him go."

Halley finished the heat-seal and let go of the gear—or tried to.

"I *can't* let him go," she said. "I'm stuck inside his pixels."

"What the hell is going on?"

Tom had stalked out from behind the house, his scowl making the lines stand out even more on his face. "What kind of service visit is this? First I find my wife on a fool's errand in our shelter, and now you have my son above your head!"

"Halley, Shmalley, made a mess..."

"Quiet, Greta." Tom jabbed a finger in Oscar's face. "I shouldn't have listened to you. This woman has no idea what she's doing."

"I'm sorry, sir, but you have to move. I need to help my apprent—"

"Help? *She is flinging my boy around like a rag doll.* The only help *she* needs is a report for gross incompetence."

"Wait, sir."

But Tom marched up to Halley. "I'm saying this one last time. *Get away from my boy.*"

Halley tried again to free herself, but she couldn't do it alone. Her hands were sunk like quicksand in the growing soup of pixels. The muscles in her hands ached. She was glad to feel them; in a few more seconds, she wouldn't have any hands to feel at all.

She turned to Tom, her eyes blazing.

"Make me," she said.

Tom roared in response. He grabbed Halley's shoulders and pulled her back. Instead of resisting, Halley leaned into him. She dug her heels into the grass, then sprang back, working with Tom's momentum.

There was a slick popping noise, and Halley's hands broke free of the pixels.

Tom spun away, but Halley watched—*blip*—as the boy appeared. Calvin landed on top of her, and they both fell in the grass.

Greta ran over. "Is she dead?"

"Alive," Oscar said, "and in one piece."

"Just like your brother," Halley said. She showed them.

Slightly dazed, Calvin sat up. He rubbed the back of his head and winced. "What the heck happened to me? I feel like I got knocked out. Did I slip during our sprinkler race?"

"Yep," Greta said. "And you lost. Big time."

"I find that hard to believe," Calvin said. "Dad, did you see who won? Dad? What's the matter? Is everything okay?"

"Everything's fine, just fine."

Tom picked up Calvin and gave him a huge hug. Afterward, he said, "Calvin, this is Halley and Oscar from the Alpha Company."

"Hello," Calvin said. "Did you come to check the vid screen in the living room? It's been pretty glitchy."

"It was," Halley said, "but we got it back online. Everything is running smoothly now, wouldn't you say?"

"No complaints here," Tom said, his voice softening. "Thank you."

"Any time."

"Hey, Mom!"

As soon as she heard the front door open, Greta skipped to the porch to break the news. "Look at Calvin, Mom. He woke up. *Finally.*"

"Oh, honey," Marion said. She nearly spilled the tray in her hands. The cup and saucer rattled against the sugar bowl, spilling very hot real tea. She recovered, thrusted the tray at Tom, and ran down to her son. She kissed him on both cheeks.

"You really are awake. Look at you. I'm so glad. And you," Marion said to Halley. "I couldn't be more grateful for you. Won't you stay for tea *and* dinner? It would be my honor."

"Geez, Mom," Calvin said, surprised. "What else did she fix beside the vid screen?"

It was early evening with a sky full of stars when the Alpha van turned off Isotope Lane. Oscar was back behind the wheel, smiling. "You knocked that one out of the park."

"You doubted me?"

"Never. You're my apprentice, aren't you? But you got something I can't teach you."

"What's that?"

"*Corazón*. And you know how to use yours. How else could you have gotten Tom mad as hell to help you? He was about ready to yank your hands out of their sockets."

"It was a good thing he got that mad. It would have been hard to shake his hand with a stump." Halley sighed. "Calvin did end up destroying my gloves when he came back online."

"Don't worry. I'll get you a replacement pair and deduct the cost from your next paycheck. I won't even charge a service fee."

"Gee, thanks." Halley glanced down at her nav chart. "Where are we going? This isn't the way to the office."

"I know."

"Mind telling me the next stop, oh great and amazing mentor?"

"Here," Oscar said, and parked.

They were in a neighborhood of Chicago-style brick apartments from the nineteenth century. The buildings were old and worn because, unlike the Division, they were built in that era. Cracks ran up the cement steps, and rust covered the iron railings.

In one ground-floor unit, the light was on in the picture window, warm and inviting. The curtain folded back, and a short, broad-faced woman peered out.

"There's Lucilia, my wife," he said. "That's our place."

"I don't understand," Halley said. "Why would you bring me to your home?"

"Why not? It's what I do for all of my apprentices who get my blessing."

"You mean—?"

"You're going up another wavelength. Ochre to avocado. You deserve it."

"I don't know what to say."

"Don't say anything. Just come on in and have some dessert. Marion's dinner was all right, I'm sure, but her kitchen made it. Nothing beats a real cup of coffee and Lucilia's *conchas*. She makes them by hand."

Oscar gave a loud, long yawn. It may have been a trick of the evening light, but his hair looked to have more salt than pepper in it. "It's been a long day today. I don't hold my charge as much as I used to."

"You might need a new battery," Halley said. "Do you need me to take a look?"

"When I get you those new gloves, sure. But not now. We're both off the clock." He opened the van door. Cool night air greeted them. "Lucilia loves it when I bring home the good ones to celebrate."

They made their way up the worn but comfortable sidewalk, two workers done for the day, all of their service stops completed, lifetimes guaranteed.

Talking and laughing, they passed through the light thrown from the picture window on their way to the front door. Oscar seemed to fade a little in that warm light, his pixels scattered like a billion motes of dust, his well-used Alpha gear floating among them. But he was still there, and still cracking dad jokes.

And Halley, her shadow cast strong and solidly behind her, laughed at every one.

M.C. St. John is the author of the short story collection Other Music. His stories have appeared in Boned, Burial Day Books, Coffin Bell, and J.J. Outré Review. See what he's writing next at www.mcstjohn.com

Ask Me About the Old Quarry

Sage Kalmus

You enter off the main road between the farm stand and the three-season shortcut into town. There used to be a parking lot there, but now it's not much more than a patch of dirt. Used to be an attendant there too, during "open hours", when that was even a thing, but I guess the town eventually figured the liability was worse with an attendant than without one. Besides, an attendant's not really practical in a place that's technically always open, is it? Or always closed, depending on your perspective. I mean, anyone can go up there. It's not like there's barbed wire and armed guards to stop you. All it's got is a ratty old sign that practically taunts: "No Jumping! No Diving!" As if a broken neck was the worst thing anyone got up there.

Point is, park anywhere. No one's looking—unless they're there for the same purpose as you, in which case, who's to judge, right? Still, I'd steer clear—especially if they're coming down the mountain and even more so if they're sopping wet. That said, personally, I'd hitch or Uber, since you don't know whether you'll even be capable of driving when you trek back down.

Regardless, once you're there, just walk straight back into the woods. Was a trail there once, but now there's no telling. Your best bet's to just keep the road square at your back and don't diverge. Keep heading up the ridge and into the forest for about a half mile. It's a mild grade, a little too mild if you ask me. I mean, maybe if it was a bit harder to get up there, more people would give up before they got the chance to go through with something they may later regret. But who am I kidding, right? You know as well as I, most folks, once they get a wild hair, there's no talking them down. I should know.

Anyway, for a while, all you'll see around you are trees and underbrush, but eventually you'll start to see little flashes of rusted metal peppering the landscape—what folks around here call the Rust Museum. Really it's just a minefield, no pun intended, of old discarded and abandoned mining equipment. Combine and excavator parts, horse hitches and rail-cart tracks—all half-buried and overgrown.

See, it isn't just a nickname. That place really is a former rock quarry. Fully operational in its time some couple-hundred odd years ago, until one day the whole crew just up and vanished. Or so the story goes. Apparently, at first the town just wrote it off as a temporary matter, like a companywide vacation or a shutdown to meet some regulatory requirement. But when it eventually came clear no one was coming back—not for the land, not even for the equipment—the town claimed eminent domain and took it all over. Filled it up with water 'cause they figured that was safer than leaving their very own Grand Canyon in deep Appalachia. Or so states the historical record. If you believe the urban legend, the hole just filled itself up with rain over time, but that would take a downpour of Biblical proportions, and the old quarry's no holy site, I'll swear to that.

I'll also suggest that, if you're even remotely curious about all those rusty artifacts scattered about up there, you check them out before you go about your way, because like I said before, once it's done, you don't know where your head's going to be at. And I mean that literally.

By now, you're right up next to the quarry, though you won't see it yet. You'll just see a trail on your right to its lower rim, while the trail you're on currently continues straight ahead where it veers sharply up to the upper rim. You won't accomplish anything jumping from the lower rim, except maybe get a pleasant day's swim—and honestly, that's my recommendation if you do anything up there at all besides take a gander. It's a sight worth seeing, truly, and you're just not going to appreciate it as much, even from high up, when you're right about to throw your actual whole life away.

It's like a little piece of paradise, it is: a pristine chasm of a lake surrounded by walls of rock shooting straight up in a rim of white, grey, brown and charcoal striations. The lake itself is fairly small, like two football fields across and a basketball court wide, but deep, is it ever! I don't think anyone ever deigned to find out, but of all I've heard over the years, I never once heard anyone say they even spotted bottom. The surface itself is like a sheet of glass, but why wouldn't it be? You get zero wind in that mammoth well. It's like a painting of itself, removed from time. Only, no painting I ever saw has that much power.

Which brings us to why you came in here, so I'll get on with it.

If, after everything I say here, you've still got your mind set, well, then, you'll have to take that other, upper trail. Because for it to work—for the thing to happen

—to leap bodies—

you've got to leap from the highest cliff.

No one knows who was the first it happened to, or what became of them. Whoever it was, though, the first to jump or dive or—even worse—trip and fall into that soulless abyss, can you imagine what must've been running through their head? How they had to feel when they resurfaced only to find themselves in someone else's skin?

I mean, you have to wonder. It's a tall leap, you'll see. Even without the body-jumping part, you'd still come up from it a bit discombobulated—you'd have to. Isn't that part of the whole draw of leaping off a cliff into a lake to begin with? You've got adrenaline and spatial disorientation, maybe some oxygen deprivation—all that. Which makes you wonder, did that first person even notice right away? Why would they? They were either out for a sunny dip or trying to kill their fool selves. Either way, not expecting anything remotely like what they got.

Imagine, you just plummeted, what, a few hundred feet into an icy bath, whether by accident or on purpose, and emerged back into fresh air. You're still catching your breath and either swimming to shore or treading water. Is that when you notice? And what would it be first? Your hands? Or something more personal, less tangible, something inside? Like, the feel of your tongue in your mouth, or how your body weight distributes differently in the water? Or is it your thoughts? They're still yours, sure, but in someone else's brain, so they've got to be different too, right? Somehow, familiar and not at all—all at the same time? Seems it would take a minute to adjust to that. So, when I think of that first person it happened to, you know what I imagine?

Screaming. Full-throttle, spitting-and-spewing, half-drowning, bloody-murder, crossing-the-border-into-insane screaming. That's how I picture it.

For all we know, that first victim may not even have made it out of that accursed lake. They easily could've kicked it right there. Actually, when you think about it, it seems the most likely possibility. In fact, I wouldn't be surprised if that's what happened to the first few, until maybe someone else was there to witness it and rescue one of those poor saps.

But whether it was the first or hundred-and-first, someone was first to make it out of that hole in a new body—or someone else's old, discarded one, more accurately. So, what must've been going through their head? Imagine if there was someone else there. How would that first conversation have gone? What could they have said? "No, it's me! I swear it! I'm me! Please, you've got to believe me!" How else could it have gone down? And how did it not wind them up in the crazy house, that first, or more likely those first few poor suckers? Even still, that old quarry is like a fast track to the nuthouse for a lot of folks. A lot of them, ones I know. Or knew, more like it.

Like my kindergarten crossing guard. Miss Nancy. It didn't happen to her until much later, though, when I was already working my first job. I hadn't heard hide nor hair of her for years, and certainly hadn't known she'd gone missing for three of them, but then one day here she comes bursting into the supermarket where I'm bagging groceries. She's screaming and completely naked, don't ask me which I noticed first. Her face is a mess. She looks like she'd literally been buried alive and dug herself out. Except she wasn't covered in dirt, she was sopping wet. Bloody bare feet, no doubt from clambering down the mountain. A sight like this was bad enough then, when I was still ignorant of all this. But knowing what I know now? I mean, who was that really in there screaming and losing her poor mind? Or his? 'Cause one thing's for certain, it wasn't Miss Nancy. Which, of course, now leaves you to wonder whatever did happen to Miss Nancy. Unfortunately, I can't answer that. But I can tell you whoever replaced her in that body blew her—or his—brains out a couple weeks later.

The first person I ever knew to make the leap was Landon Easterbrook, a kid I knew in middle school. We weren't exactly friends, more like acquaintances, and as it turned out, we'd never get the chance to get any closer. I wasn't there the day it happened but some of my friends were. We had all heard the stories about the place. It was like our own local haunted house. Kids were always daring each other to jump. But no one knew anyone who actually took up that dare. At least no one I knew of, until Landon.

Apparently, the scrawny, pimple-faced nerd felt he had something to prove. The dude that came up looked about 35 and like he had nothing to prove to no one. He seemed shell-shocked, is how my friends described it, like he'd been through an explosion. One of the original miners, was always my thinking. In any case, last I heard, poor Landon's still in prison for his own kidnapping. Heard he spent his whole trial and sentencing defiant, though, swearing up and down that someday someone else would get spotted in his old skin and exonerate him. I wonder if he's still so optimistic.

The one time I ever saw with my own eyes what happens there, I was with my cousins. There were three of us. We were planning to take turns jumping. I was supposed to be second to go, but we never got that far. Down went my one cousin, Wade, and up came this haggard, beefy guy we later found out was a registered sex offender. While he wailed in a quivering, heaving heap on the shoreline, bedraggled and confused, my aunt and uncle were calling 911 in a panic over their drowned child. Before long, there were police, ambulances, helicopters up there, it was a mess. Cousin Wade, or the creep he was stuck in now, was hauled away in the back of a squad car. You could still hear his terrified howl—a little boy's wail in a full-grown man's voice—as the car trundled down the dirt trail and out of distance. It was the last I heard of Cousin Wade, and the last time I socialized with that part of the family, unless you count Cousin Wade's funeral. Of course, they had to bury an empty casket.

The worst, I think, was this whole family: the Cartwrights. Eight of the nine kids, the father and the babysitter. One by one, or in some cases in pairs, they all took the leap, none of them ever knowing what was in store for them. A few even came up as each other, including the youngest who came up as her father. From what I understand, that was the straw that broke the whole clan's back, seeing the pillar of the family reduced to a blubbering little girl. Even the mother, whose aquaphobia kept her safely several feet from the water at all times, and the one child who didn't yet know how to swim wound up with the rest of them at the local asylum. I'm still not sure who I feel worse for, the ones who lost themselves by becoming someone else or the ones who lost themselves by watching the ones they loved disappear before their eyes.

Now, obviously plenty of folks do make it down off that mountain in something other than a stretcher, straightjacket or body bag. Some, in fact, have the exact opposite outcome. Mind you, these are mostly the folks who did it on purpose, in full awareness of what to expect. And as you might expect, these were mostly folks very low on hope with nothing much to live for, at least as they saw it, except of course for a stubborn unwillingness—whether from fear or pride—to simply kill themselves and be done with it. For a lot of folks it's the holy grail—a third option. Not quite death, not quite life—or at least not the same life. The person who had it before is clearly done with it, so it's yours guilt-free for the taking to do with what you want. For some, the temptation is too great. They see it as a free pass—though I'm not so sure about the "free" part.

Like this stranger who rolled into town once in the back of a police wagon. No ID, no fingerprint or DNA records. Cops said they found him wandering the roads gape-eyed and rambling to himself. Now he teaches computer skills at the vocational school in town. Regular schools won't hire him since he obviously can't pass a background check. Who was he before? Why'd he take the leap? Does he or doesn't he remember? If he does, he's not telling.

But why would he, right? Who goes through all that for a second chance only to keep dredging the past back up?

I think that's why most folks who take the plunge skip town as soon as they can. That and there's always the chance of running into someone who knew the person whose body you're now occupying. Can you say awkward?

Like the old chief of police. Went for a hike and a swim on his day off and came back a new man, only for real. Rumor has it the station was in chaos for a week as the imposter tried to play off being chief. It seems incredible to me it took a force of trained detectives a week to figure out their chief wasn't their chief anymore, but who knows? Maybe that uniform's previous occupant was completely incompetent too. Maybe that's why he jumped. People who dismiss "the whole quarry thing" altogether believe he probably just hit his head on a rock on the way down and came up stupid. More likely, some overemotional junior high schooler landed in his skin. In any case, now he pumps gas at a freeway pitstop on the graveyard shift. And I haven't heard anyone yet going around claiming to be the former chief of police. But I'm waiting.

So, you see, some folks live a whole new life post-leap in perfect contentment. You don't hear as much about them, mind you, but that's probably just the nature of leading contented lives. They're not like the ones who keep coming back, something always breaking their stride—cancer, divorce—and bringing them back to that precipice.

'Cause you can always go again, if you're really unhappy with the new you the first time. Like if you're old and come up older, or sick and come up sicker. Or you come up as a draft dodger up for court martial or an accused murderer wanted by the FBI. You go again, and again if necessary, until you get it right. Just not during the winter, though.

It seems obvious, I know, but every year some fool leaps after the first frost and breaks their neck on the ice. So, if it's the end of autumn, you will have to tough it out til spring. But otherwise, you can keep trading yourself in for a different model like a used car as often as you want. Of course, there's consequences. The more you jump, the harder it is to hold onto yourself. And that's not just rumor either. I know from personal experience.

After a really big fight with Robin, my girlfriend at the time, when I said some things I shouldn't have, she took the leap and came up a dude. Not an old or decrepit one, mind you, and not even a bad-looking one—on a purely objective level. Didn't have a warrant out for his arrest, as far as we could tell, and no serious medical conditions. But none of that mattered to her. She couldn't handle being male—or no longer being female, possibly. Either way, she hadn't accounted for that. I tried to tell her it didn't matter, though I don't know how convincing I was. I mean, of course it mattered, huge! I don't swing that way, but we would've figured something out. Apparently, for Robin, that wasn't good enough.

I don't blame her for ending the relationship, really. I just wish it could've solved her problem. But I guess being a girl in a boy's body eventually got to be too much for her and, last I heard, she jumped again—and came up a dude again, big shocker. Apparently there are a lot more male bodies down there than female ones—someone should do a study. In any case, she jumped again and again, so many times I eventually lost track. Apparently, she did too. With every jump she had a harder and harder time holding onto Robin and sorting out all the other people she'd been for a minute. She could be anyone now. She could be you, could be the President. In any case, she's not telling me.

People try, God bless 'em. They try so hard to hit the refresh button on their lives. But it's harder than most think. Some folks, a lot of folks, can't get out of their own way enough to be anyone else. Not even for a minute, let alone a lifetime. Folks spend so damn much time fixed on what they're running from—themselves, their lives, their failures and mistakes—they never give much thought at all to where or what it is they're running to. Of course, when a person gets to that point of leaping, chances are they don't much care where they land. Saddest are those like my ex, Robin—I call them the regretters—who keep leaping in the hopes of getting back

what they lost. As far as I know, there's no backsies. At least, I never heard anyone claim different.

No one knows why the quarry does what it does. Folks got plenty of theories, mind you, myself included. Mine is the miners never actually abandoned the quarry, not in the traditional sense at least—on their own two feet. That instead they struck something down there they weren't expecting. Unburied something meant to stay buried, and that, whatever it was, it put their bodies into some sort of limbo. Maybe an avalanche trapped them in until the water came. Whatever the case, it would explain why there were so many bodies at the ready when people started dropping down there, why people aren't just coming up as the last one to leap right before them. There's generations of bodies, I reckon, just floating down there waiting for a soul to claim them. The way I picture it, when a person leaps, they must inhabit whatever body they happen to snag first on the way down.

Little Landon Easterbrook may have been the first person I ever knew of to suffer the fate of the old quarry when it happened, but the first time I ever saw that fate with my own eyes was long before I ever even knew what I was looking at. It was a few days after my dad walked out on my mom. Suddenly, this strange guy moves into the house like he's taking over. At first we thought our mom just brought him home from the bar, but it soon became clear she didn't want him there either. She didn't do anything about it, though. She wouldn't call the police, and wouldn't let us either, even after he started hitting her. Craziest thing was this new guy acted just like our father. We figured that's why she let him stay there, 'cause he felt familiar. How were we to know, right?

Soon after, my older brother ran away and never came back. Years later—side story—I was on a trip in Reno and this waitress hands me a note with an old childhood joke my brother always used to tell and he'd always flub the same part—just like in the note. I looked everywhere for him...her, after that. But her coworkers said she'd up and quit right then, and I knew that was the last I'd ever see of her... him.

As for the rest of us, mom eventually couldn't take it anymore and moved us a town over. She did her best at a disguise, throwing herself off that cliff and coming up some pot-bellied dude with a cleft palate and shingles. Turns out it didn't even matter, 'cause our new old man eventually got tired of chasing his past and went on to start a whole new family. Same house, same life. Like he literally started over. Like hitting replay on the same record. He didn't need a whole new body for that.

In any event, if systematically losing everyone I ever loved to that old rockpit had any positive outcome for me, it's that I got a sort of second chance of my own out of it. See, my old boss, Mr. Heller, the former proprietor of this inn, had faced the same dilemma as me. One by one, his wife and all his kids took the leap. Only difference between us was I didn't ultimately follow my kin off that ledge. I was already working here vacuuming floors and changing linens when he decided he couldn't endure it any longer. He never said what was the clincher for him, but I'm betting one of his daughters tried to check in one night and didn't even recognize him. Well, by then Mr. Heller was already calling me his second son, but I wonder if giving me the place was more about seeing himself in me than it was any paternal motivations. Whatever the case, he spared me returning to show what became of him, and for that above all else I'm forever grateful.

I empathize, believe me. With old man Heller who left me his legacy to chase a family he no longer had, with my former friends and family, with folks like you seeking second chances—desperate enough to take whatever you can get. But I don't think I'd ever take that bet—call it strength, call it cowardice, whatever you like. I've had plenty of opportunity, believe me, been up there more than I care to count. First time just to check it out, see it with my own eyes. A bunch of times after to babysit my friends, keep them from making a bad decision they could never undo. Been called up there a few times to rescue a friend once it was already too late. Honestly, sometimes I'd just go up there to swim, but no more. Too many memories of people gone, or forever changed, which is really the same thing. But if I'm honest, I don't think I've ever been seriously tempted to jump. Not because I think I'm so great or my life is so perfect, far from it. But at least my problems are my own, right? Why would I want to stick myself with anyone else's? Especially when I start thinking about who's all bobbing around down there. Like my dad and mom. My brother. My cousin Wade. Robin. Landon Easterbrook. The Hellers. I'd rather mourn them than chance becoming them, you know?

So I do this instead. I posted that sign out front and I tell this same story to anyone, like you, who follows its advice. I don't have a keychain or a postcard of the place to peddle, but I will tell you what you'll find there, and that's more than anyone else around here will do. I mean, I don't blame them. Most aren't themselves anymore, so they've got too much to protect. But someone's got to let people know what goes on up there before they go getting into something they can't get back from.

So, now that you know what happens there, it's your call what to do with the information. Just remember, there's plenty of ways to start over. But once you give it over to the old quarry, whoever you are now is gone forever. So you've got to ask yourself: is it really worth throwing it all away? 'Cause you can get all the second chances you want, but there are no do-overs. And when you close your eyes and fall asleep at night, there's still only you—the real you—and only you to contend with it.

It's not my place to act like I know what's best for anyone, so I'm the last person to tell you not to do it. But I will say this: if you do go through with it, don't come back here after. Please do me that one courtesy. Settle your bill before you go and take your belongings with you. What you do with them is your business—though, truthfully, if you do go through with it, what happens to your stuff will be the least of your concerns.

If you need, there's a bar up at the five corners where you'll find plenty of ears to bend. It's where I used to go for years after clocking out of here, until it got too hard—

every familiar face now a stranger and every stranger swearing you know them.

On the other hand, if after you've thought it through, you decide not to take that leap and you want to sit down and share a few brews with someone who doesn't know or much care what you're running from, you know where to find me.

Sage Kalmus is a Pushcart-Prize-nominated writer whose work has appeared in "The Writer", "Spine Magazine", the anthology "Sanctuary", "Whisperings Magazine", "Carnival Online Literary Journal" and "Rose Red Review" as well as "Queer Families: LGBTQ+ True Stories Anthology" which he also edited. His latest publication, "Burning Monkfish" is a finalist in the Defenestrationism.net 2020 !Short Story Contest (their punctuation.) He holds a creative writing MFA from Lesley University where he teaches a course in writing magical realism.

The Call of the Wyld

Twelve grisly tales of fur and fury in this brand new anthology of werewolf stories from Wyldblood press.

- Werewolves on the prowl!
- Werewolves at your door!
- Werewolves in space!
- Werewolves in your nightmares!

Out now £7.99 print £3.99 ebook
www.wyldblood.com/bookstore.

Plumes

Regina Higgins

California, 1873

She was in the water, letting the ocean waves carry her to shore when I first saw her. I was standing on the beach, hand over my eyes against the glare. The sun was setting right behind the girl.

I walked down to the surf as she was wading in. Her clothes, all but the cap she was wearing, were in a heap on the sand. She was reaching for them as I came near, and she didn't see me, I guess. That, or she was shy. Anyway, she startled when she saw me.

"Whatcha doing here?" I asked.

I didn't say it in a "be off with you!" way. At least I hoped not. I really was curious about her. She was maybe thirteen years old, pale, wide-eyed, very slim.

She pulled her dress on, and I saw it was very fine, what Lizzie would call "quality." But it was torn at the hem and stained here and there, like she'd be travelling in it too long.

"I'm Tilda," I told her. "Short for Matilda." I stuck out my hand for a shake.

She took my hand and squeezed it just a bit. Then her pretty green eyes rolled back and she slumped to the sand. The little cap fell off, and saw the mass of red-gold she'd hidden underneath.

I slung her over my shoulder easily—she was a tiny thing—gathered up her clothes and her boots and cap and carried her from the beach up the hill and back to the ranch. It wasn't far, and, like I said, she was a little one.

As soon as we arrived at the cabin, the whole crew started getting blankets and pulling the best cot out and putting on water to boil for tea.

Once the bed was ready, I placed her gently down. Oona smoothed the plumpest pillow and slipped it under her head.

"She's beautiful," Oona said. "Where did you find her?"

That made Lizzie laugh. "She's not a knick-knack, you know."

Kitty pushed them both aside.

"Out of the way."

Kitty leaned over the bed and put her hand to the girl's forehead. She's been a nurse back East.

"Seems okay. Looks like she just fainted," she said.

"Poor kid," Lizzie whispered.

Kitty felt the girl's arms and looked carefully at her fingers. "She's been well cared for until recently. You can tell from her hair and her hands."

We were all bedazzled by the shiny red-gold curls, for sure. Then Kitty showed us her fingernails, short but not broken.

"Good nutrition and no hard labor."

"Then what was she doing on the beach all alone?" I asked her.

Kitty looked at her and shook her head. "Probably ran away."

"That explains the *soignée* dress," Lizzie said. She picked up one of the girl's boots. "Quality leather. But it looks like she's been on the road. There's deep scratches, you see here--"

Kitty broke in. "It's obvious she's been walking quite a way, from the look of the clothes. And that would explain the fainting, too. Exhaustion." She pulled out her pocket watch and put two fingers to the girl's throat. After a minute, she nodded. "Yep. I'd say this girl's just tired, hungry, and lost."

"Well, we can help with that," I said. "She can stay here with us. We could always use an extra hand."

Oona gave me a straight look. "This little girl is used to living like a lady. How do you think she'll like living on a ranch?"

"I was a banker's daughter back East," Lizzie pointed out. "She may like it here."

Oona shook her head. "I expect she won't particularly take to ranch work. Picture her in jeans and rough boots, forking out the hay? Or mucking out the stables?"

Lizzie just laughed. "We'll see."

None of us knew, of course. But the more I looked at her, the more I could imagine her in a broad-brimmed hat, whooping as she rode. She had spirit. She'd run away from the rich, lounging kind of life. And she'd run away alone. A girl like that is strong.

The girl finally woke up about midnight. She opened those bright green eyes and looked at us crowded around her cot.

Kitty crouched by the side of the cot and spoke very quietly.

"Miss," she said, "are you comfortable? Do you have any pain?"

The girl gazed at her and answered in a whisper.

"No. I'm alright."

Kitty leaned in closer.

"Can you tell us your name?"

"I'm Emma," she said, a little louder than before.

"Emma what?"

"Just Emma." She lifted her head and struggled to sit up.

"Lie down for now," said Kitty, and she gently touched her arm.

Then I spoke. "Where are you from, Emma? Where's your home?"

She was quiet for a long time, and I could see her eyes flickering all around, taking in the rough wood walls, the stone fireplace, the narrow cots. Then she looked up at me—at all of us.

"I want to stay here."

I grew up on this spread. Pop taught me to ride and rope and care for the horses and all the rest when I was just little. Well, he had no choice. We were alone, Pop and me, so I had to help. We were a kind of livery for the whole town, so we were busy. Usually had about ten or so horses in the corral. People were always coming by, getting their horses or dropping them off, or hiring ours.

I loved waking up early and feeding the horses, exercising them, currying them, and all. I loved going out to the corral and feeling them nuzzle me as I led them out to pasture. I loved riding them, and roping, when they got too frisky or started to stray. It was a good life. And as Pop said, "if you can pay the bills doing something you love, you're probably the luckiest fellow in the world."

All the town folks treated me fine. Like I knew what I was doing, which I did, of course. But when Pop died suddenly—I was sixteen—everyone just figured I'd be leaving the ranch, going off to live with some relative or other somewhere.

Nope.

Or I'd get a lawyer to help me sell the place and then move to town.

Again, nope.

Or—and lots of folks were real sure about this—I'd marry quick and stay on or sell, but be the rancher's wife and not the rancher.

Hell, nope.

I was going to stay, and on my own terms. When folks heard this, they just shook their heads and waited for me to get over my craziness.

I wasn't the least bit crazy. I knew I could make a go of it. But I also knew I needed help to run the place, just like Pop had. So I thought a lot about who I might want to help me, and then I wrote out an advertisement to put in the local newspaper. And, for good measure, I sent it to lots of other papers, too. St. Louis. Chicago. Kansas City. Even New York and Boston.

Cowgirl Roundup!

We're looking for you! Ready to work or willing to learn, able to rope, ride, herd on the finest spread on earth. Good food, good company. Forget the office, forget the mill. Tell the boss to jump out the window. You're not a typewriter, you're a cowgirl! Saddle up and head out here. We'll be waiting.

And, what do you know, they came. Lizzie the debutante and Oona the shopgirl and Kitty the nurse. They came and they stayed, trading their fancy dresses for shirts and jeans and boots, their city ways for ranch life and work.

Everyone around here still thought I was crazy. But when they saw we were running the place well, taking care of their horses just like before, and making a living at it, they left us alone.

The "making a living" part was touch and go, although the town didn't know that. Taxes were due every quarter, twenty-five dollars in cash. So far we'd made it, only just. But the price of feed for the horses was going up and food was getting more expensive. I spent a lot of time awake at night, adding and subtracting and worrying. One missed tax payment meant we'd lose the ranch.

And then Emma showed up. Though we didn't know it then, everything was about to change.

The first morning, Emma put on the shirt and jeans and boots that Lizzie put by her cot, and sat right down with us for coffee and biscuits. Because she was so little, I thought I'd start her out slow. So I put her in charge of cooking dinner while we were out working with the horses.

And she did well. Baked a fine pie and cooked up some pretty tasty stew. Even Oona had to admit that if the little girl was brought up to be a lady, she must have spent quite some time in the kitchen with a first-class cook.

But Emma was set on trying her hand at riding, roping, and the rest. Every morning, when she was done with the washing up, she'd follow us out, stand at a distance, and just watch us with the horses.

One evening after supper, I grabbed my lariat and called to her.

"Come on, Em," I said. "Let's try some roping."

When we got to what the girls called "Tilda's roping place" by the corral, just about eight feet from a handy post, I showed Emma the lariat and showed her how to make a loop. Then I gave the little talk I always gave the girls when they were going to learn to rope. It's how Pop taught me when I was just a kid. You don't *throw* the rope, Pop told me. You *release* it. Big difference.

I showed Emma how to swing it over your head to get the energy going. And then—now this is up to you, I told her— you feel it's ready to release. That's when you swing it towards your target, the post near the corral, and the loop goes flying through the air (I showed her) and as soon as it's there at the target—boom!—you pull on the lariat and, well, whatever it is, it's roped.

I showed her a couple of times and then handed her the lariat. I left her there by the post and walked back to the cabin, where the girls were watching from the porch.

"Took me more teaching than that," Oona told me as I passed by.

"Well, we'll see." I turned to look back at Emma whirling the loop over her head. "Let's leave her to it, anyway."

So we all went inside and played some po ker. Lizzie was dealer and with each

hand she had some crazy idea, aces or jacks wild, or something else. Oona and Kitty played along fine, but I guess I was distracted. Finally I just threw down my cards and gave up. I stood to look out the window.

"She still at it?" Kitty asked.

"I could just barely see Emma in the moonlight by the corral. She was whirling the lariat over her head—very well, I had to admit—then releasing and pulling.

But did she have a target? I couldn't make it out. From what I could see, she was turning in a different direction each time, almost like she was dancing.

She released and pulled again and again. Then she suddenly jumped through the loop and back again. Through the loop and back, one, two, three, four times. And one time just after she'd jumped through the loop I couldn't see her at all. Where did she go?

Then she was back there again, twirling away. She released and jumped through the loop (where was she?) and back again.

And then she did it again. I could hear her laughing out there in the moonlight.

That's when I decided it was time for me to turn in.

The next morning, after she'd cleared up the breakfast dishes, Emma told me flat out "I'm going for a walk." And out the door she went.

No looking for an invitation to tag along while we worked with the horses. Just "see you" and bam, she was gone.

Out in the pasture, I kept looking over my shoulder, sure I'd see her trailing us, just like always. But nope. No sign of her.

Kitty noticed, too. "Where's the little one this morning?"

I shrugged. "Out for a walk, she said."

Kitty nodded in thought. "That's good. Good for her." She turned and rode off to chase after a roan mare who was wandering a bit too far off.

We came back to the cabin for dinner at noon and found the table all set and the stew ready. But no Emma. While the girls sat down and dug in, I went looking around outside for her. Wasn't worried, really. Well, maybe a little.

I thought I heard someone singing round back of the cabin. Turned the corner and there she was, standing next to a six-foot ostrich, just singing and stroking his feathers. The bird saw me first. He glared and started to lift his big black and white wings. Trying to frighten me off, I guess. But Emma soothed him with her song. After a moment he tossed his head at me (who cares for you?) and turned away.

"Isn't he a beauty?" Emma said, stroking his feathers.

"Where'd he come from?" I asked. "You find him on your walk?"

"He was over there." She pointed to the hills in the east, about a mile or so off. "There was a sort of tumble-down cabin, and he was wandering around nearby. He followed me home. Those ones, too."

She nodded to her right and I saw five female ostriches ruffling their gray feathers and picking in the dirt, looking for, I don't know, probably seeds and bugs.

I knew that cabin. Nobody owned it that I knew. Not since old man Ferguson died, and he didn't have any family. People would use it as they were passing through. They'd stay a few months and then move on. The ostriches must have been abandoned by someone, I guessed.

"So, what'll you do with them?" I asked Emma.

"I'll let them graze," she told me, arm on the big bird's back.

I put on what I hoped she'd see was a serious face. "Emma," I said, "this is a ranch. We don't keep pets here. They've got to earn their keep. Now, what are you going to do with these birds?"

She looked at me, puzzled. "Don't you know?"

Just then the male ostrich—the Big Guy, I thought of him—stretched his wings wide. And suddenly a long, full dark-as-night black feather floated to the ground.

Emma stooped to pick it up. She smiled and waved it before me.

"We sell these."

When we went into the cabin together, the girls were still at the table, gobbling stew and grabbing for biscuits. Only Lizzie looked up and saw Emma waving that big fluffy feather.

Lizzie dropped her spoon. "Where'd you find that?" She reached out a hand. "That's an ostrich plume, isn't it?"

Emma smiled and handed her the feather. "There's a ton more outside, walking around."

Now everybody was up and out the door, Emma leading them around the back. And there they were. Those birds were still scraggling around for food.

Oona whistled. "Some sight."

"Can we keep 'em?" Kitty asked. She shyly stroked one of the females.

Emma brought the bird closer and showed Kitty how to pet her.

"That depends," I told Kitty. Then, very quietly, I asked Lizzie, "D'ya think we could see those feathers? I mean, could we make it worth our while?"

Lizzie smiled at that. "Oh, yeah."

"But how?"

She picked up a white plume and tucked it in her dark hair. "Millinery."

"What?"

"Ladies' hats!" She laughed. "The milliners in all the little towns around here will pay top dollar for these." Kitty nodded, and the feather in her hair gently waved. "You'll see."

The next week Emma and Lizzie kept busy gathering and sorting feathers, making plans I didn't entirely understand. Because Lizzie insisted the feathers would bring in cash, something we could use more of at any time, we gave those big old birds a place in the corral, where the horses watched them with a wary eye. Good thing they (the birds, I mean) seemed to be able to find their own food around the place, shrubs and seeds and bugs, and all.

One morning Emma and Lizzie came into the cabin with baskets full of berries.

"Are you going to bake a pie?" I asked. I hoped so.

But nope. "This is to dye the feathers," Emma told me. She pulled out three metal pans.

"Huckleberries for light purple," Kitty explained, "blueberries for a dark blue, and raspberries for pink." She dumped the berries in the pans and went at them with a wooden masher we usually used for potatoes.

I shook my head and walked out. Bumped into Oona on the porch.

"What's going on in there?"

I shrugged. "Putting colors on those feathers to sell. From berries."

"Good idea!" Oona said. She leaned a bit to get a look inside.

I just shook my head again. "If they're going to all the trouble to pick berries, I'd rather have a pie."

Oona laughed. "You'll see."

I hoped I would. Quarterly taxes were due soon, and we were short by seventeen dollars. I'd feel a lot better about the birds if they could bring us in that money. Otherwise, I'd have to lay down the law and tell Emma they weren't worth our time. I hate being the bad guy, but facts are facts.

A few days later Lizzie and Emma hitched horses to the wagon and headed off to town with their feathers to show to the hat lady there. They'd tucked them safe in some burlap bags so they wouldn't blow away on the road. Good thinking. But what if she doesn't want to buy them?

I put on a show of cheeriness, though. "Good luck!" I called, waving so long to them as they headed out. And then, just because I couldn't help it, I yelled, "Hope you sell them for a good price!"

"We intend to!" Lizzie shouted over her shoulder.

I was pretty busy that day, as it happened. Couple of folks came by to stable their horses and another came looking to borrow a gelding for some ploughing. Just one thing and the other all day long.

But when I had a moment now and then, I thought about hats and all the crazy things about them. Pop had a nice felt one made for me, no doodads, or anything, and it suits me fine. Why would anyone want to put stuff on their hat—those feathers, I mean. What do you do when it gets all wet and tangled and dirty? How do you clean a hat like that? When my hat gets dusty, I just take it off and whomp it against my knee. Good as new. But what do you do with a hat full of feathers and such? I guess there's some things I'll just never understand.

It was nearly dark and I was making sure all the horses—and those silly damn birds—were in the corral when Oona came running up to me.

"They're back!" she shouted. "That hat lady bought all the feathers! And they've got twenty-five dollars in gold!"

That's how we paid the taxes that quarter. And the hat lady ordered some more feathers and told her sister the dressmaker about us, so we got an order from her, too. And that sister had a hat lady friend in Sacramento who also had a dressmaker friend, and so on. Before you knew it, Emma and Lizzie were busy picking and dyeing feathers from dawn to dusk, trying to keep up with the orders.

So now the birds were paying their way and more, and the ranch became the place to come for all your hoof or feather needs. Sometimes both.

Our local undertaker heard all the fuss about the feathers. When he came to get his horses for a funeral, he asked if he could have some big, black plumes for them.

"For fancy funerals," he told us, "the horses have them on their heads. And folks appreciate little things like that." He smiled. "And they're willing to pay for them, too."

Well, sure, I said, and I called Emma over. That girl had some great ostrich-wrangling skills, I told him. And it was true. She'd walk right over to them, humming or singing, loop one arm around their neck and gently feel for loose feathers with the other. If she didn't find any, she'd slip a little clipper from her pocket—still singing—and snip a feather higher than the root, so it wouldn't hurt and would grow back. Made it look like there was nothing to it.

It wasn't five minutes before Emma was walking over with four big, black plumes from the Big Guy for the undertaker's horses. He went away happy, and we got an extra ten dollars on top of the livery fee because, Emma told him, they were the *best* feathers.

After the undertaker left, I thanked Emma.

She smiled. "The birds are working out on the ranch, aren't they? Pulling their weight, I mean?"

"No doubt about it," I had to admit. "And I'll tell you something else. I do believe you love those birds just as much as I love the horses."

Emma stroked the Big Guy's back. "Well," she whispered. "I think I do."

What a strange girl, I thought right then. Where had she come from, anyway?

After that, you just couldn't stop folks from coming by the ranch to gawp at the ostriches. That wasn't exactly popular with the birds, though. Emma tried to keep them calm for everybody's safety, but some folks just have to get close to something they like, I guess. The lady hatter's husband tried to pet the Big Guy, and got himself a great big ostrich kick in the gut for it. I could have sworn I saw the horses laughing over that one. They always kept their distance from the Big Guy. Horses are smart.

And we got orders by mail. Our undertaker had a friend in San Francisco and he wanted plumes for his funeral horses, too, just like his buddy had.

The day the letter from San Francisco arrived, Lizzie pulled me aside to show me. She opened all the mail and Emma kept the books. That how they'd arranged it.

"Well, it looks worthwhile to me," I said when I'd read the order. Very heavy, fancy paper, I might add. I read it aloud. "Special funeral for a rich girl, he wants a good show. Shame she's dead." I handed her back the letter. "But why are you showing me this?"

"He mentions he wants the feathers delivered in person. And the letter is addressed to Emma," Kitty pointed out.

"Well, what's the problem? Emma can go to San Francisco, and you can take care of things here for a few days. Do you not want to do that?"

Lizzie frowned and shook her head a bit. "It's this," she said. "It was included in the letter."

She handed me a newspaper clipping about the girl—the dead girl. It wasn't like a regular death notice, with the dates and parents and all. It was more like a news story.

San Francisco Chronicle
June 12, 1873

Lawrence Calvert, Esq. and his sister Mrs. Adele Simpson have been arrested for the murder of Elizabeth Collins, the fourteen-year-old daughter of the late Ezra Collins, one of our city's most prominent bankers and investors. The young girl is believed to have died from poisoning at the hands of Calvert and Simpson.

Calvert served as Collins' legal and financial advisor, taking charge of the banker's affairs during a period of ill health. Both Calvert and his sister moved into the family home shortly before Collins' death last month. Ostensibly, they were in residence to better support their employer's business affairs and to care for his young daughter.

Collins suffered from heart disease, but, according to his physician, his death was not related to his condition. A week after Collins' death, his daughter and sole heir suddenly succumbed as well, collapsing in her bedroom shortly after supper.

According to the cook, that evening Calvert had brought a jar of bilberry preserves to the table, pressing the young girl to taste it. When the cook heard that the young lady had fallen ill after supper, he scraped the remaining preserves from her plate and brought it to police. It was found to contain arsenic.

Readers may remember the unaccountable disappearance several years

71

ago of the young Emma Swanson, daughter of the late George Swanson, Esq., shortly after her father's sudden death. It may be no coincidence that Calvert and his sister were also in residence at the Swanson house when those unfortunate incidents occurred.

I suddenly felt cold all over. Then Lizzie said just what I was thinking.

"Could it be our Emma? The Emma who disappeared?"

I shrugged.

Lizzie went on. "Should we show Emma the clipping and ask if it's her? She may not want to go to San Francisco if it is."

"No." I was sure as sure we shouldn't do that. If we asked Emma, and she was the girl who'd disappeared, I was worried she'd lie and say no. And I didn't want to hear a lie from her. And, even more, I didn't want to scare her into a lie. She'd never trust us again if that happened. I was sure.

"Let's give her the order but not the clipping," I told Lizzie. "We'll ask her if she thinks it's worth the trip." I handed Lizzie the clipping. "And then we'll see what she says."

Emma was at the table, making a note in her order book when we came in. She looked up and smiled at us.

"Howdy," she said, closing the book. "Just entered the payments from last week. Fourteen dollars, including the plume the hat lady chose for herself."

"That's great, Emma," I told her. But something in my voice must have given me away.

Emma looked at me with a little frown. "Something wrong?"

"Not a bit," Lizzie said. She waved the envelope. "Got another order. Big one, too."

Emma laughed and clapped her hands at that.

"In San Francisco," Lizzie told her. "And he's asked you to come there personally."

Lizzie sat down at the table and slid the letter over for Emma to see.

At "San Francisco" I thought I saw Emma's smile fade. And when she heard she'd have to go there, I'm almost sure I saw her pale.

Lizzie had given her the letter, but not the clipping. Emma read it carefully. As she did, I shot Lizzie a glance. She shrugged slightly and looked away. She wasn't sure, either.

"It's a big order, alright," Emma said at last. "More than what we cleared the last two weeks." She folded the letter again and looked up at us. "It'd be foolish to pass it up. If we impress him this time, we might be the regular supplier. And San Francisco—that's a big market."

Well, I thought, you are one hell of a poker player, girl.

Lizzie pressed on. "You'd have to go to San Francisco, though," she pointed out.

Emma nodded—and again, complete poker face. "That's time and money. And you'd have the other orders we've got to prepare by yourself. So, there's that to consider."

I thought I'd try to break through. "Sad about the poor little girl who's died . . . "

Emma picked up the letter again. "Wasn't she rich?"

I looked over at Lizzie and shook my head.

"It's getting late," Emma said as she put the letter back in the envelope. "Let's give it some thought, sleep on it, and decide tomorrow. I'll check on the birds while it's still light. Might find a plume or two while I'm at it.

And with that she strode out the door into the twilight. She was headed toward the corral, but the birds didn't stretch their wings and prance around like they usually did when she came near. I think I saw her with the lariat, whirling a loop over her head and to the side. And then I couldn't see her at all.

The next morning Lizzie woke me with the news that the San Francisco order—all of it—had been prepared and was ready to be delivered.

"Good work," I told her with a yawn. "You and Emma must have been up very late."

"No, you don't understand," she told me. "I went to bed. Emma must've done it all."

"Well, then, good for her," I said. "I don't blame her for sleeping late this morning."

"No," Lizzie told me again. "She's not sleeping late. She's not here. She's gone."

I slung myself out from under the covers and walked over to Emma's cot. It was smoothed and made up, with a dozen or more black feathers neatly laid out on it. On the pillow was a note.

Dear Tilda and all,

Here's the order. I've included several appropriate black plumes for him to choose from. So that should make him happy.

Don't take less than the amount he mentioned in the letter ($50).

I'm moving on. Thanks for everything.

Best,

Cassady

P.S. I'm Cassady now.

"Well, shoot," I said. "Where'd she go? Do you think she's coming back?"

Lizzie gave me a straight look. "Of course not. You know that."

While we drank coffee, all of us talked about what to do about the order. Since Lizzie was the only one who'd been working with the big birds, we figured she'd stay at the ranch while Oona went to San Francisco with the order. That would leave us a little short-handed with the horses, but the money, we agreed, would more than make up for the inconvenience.

"That's the next six months of taxes paid right there," Kitty pointed out.

So, of course, we were going ahead with the order. But we were all still wondering what would become of Emma, though we didn't say anything about it.

Kitty came the closest. After she read the note again, she nodded and said, "Cassady's a good name for her. She's a strong girl."

There was plenty of work for us, with Emma gone and Oona off to San Francisco. The horses behaved themselves, which was lucky for Kitty and me. But the birds were pretty rowdy. Lonesome for Emma, no doubt. And Lizzie just didn't have the touch with them that Emma had. After getting kicked hard about half a dozen times, Lizzie flat gave up.

"I can't do it," she told me, rubbing a sore thigh. "They're just too much for me."

I understood, of course. But what were we going to do with the birds? I asked around town if anyone would be interested in buying them, or just plain taking them off our hands. Nope. I made a big point of how they could make money with the feathers. And I mentioned an idea Emma had had about selling the eggs as curiosities. Again, nope. I even went to the dining room of the hotel and told them they could be the talk of the county if they'd take on the birds and start serving special Giant Ostrich Egg breakfasts. Still nope, with a side of "I think I know how to run my own business" and a polite order to leave and never come back.

So, what to do? I was out of ideas.

That night, I had a dream, a strange one. I don't usually have dreams, or at least I don't remember them. But this one was different.

I was standing on the beach and Emma was in the surf, just like the first time I saw

her. I was waving and calling to her. She turned and looked at me. Then she dove into a wave and swam away—I could just see her red gold curls. She'd seen me, but she kept swimming. It seemed as if she was headed way out to sea.

I woke up in a sweat. That dream shook me, I tell you. But there were chores to do. Most of all, there was the problem of what to do with those birds.

That morning, I sat drinking coffee until everyone else had finished breakfast and gone out to work. I guess they could see I didn't want to talk. Then when I was ready, I got up, went to the birds in the corral, and led them out. I leashed the Big Guy first and the rest just followed.

I walked them through the hills and up to Old Man Ferguson's cabin, where Emma had found them. It was abandoned, still. I guess I half-expected Emma to be there. But she wasn't.

I unleashed the Big Guy.

"Stay here, now," I whispered to him. "Don't follow me."

I began to walk off, and had a feeling that the Big Guy was behind me. I turned to check, and there he was, loping along in my footsteps.

"Go 'way!" I told him. "Shoo!"

The Big Guy stood his ground and glared at me. Then he turned away, ruffled his big wings, and strode off.

I thought of the Bible verse about shaking the dust from your sandals when you leave a place that doesn't welcome you. I almost wish he'd kicked me instead.

Since then, things have returned to a kind of normal on the ranch. We work with the horses every day and we've got a little savings from the feathers, so we're not so nervous about the taxes. People come by and ask about Emma and the birds, and we just say they've moved on. That's all we know, anyway.

Sometimes when I'm on the beach, I remember my dream. I know it sounds crazy, but I look for Emma in the surf, swimming out towards the open sea. A little girl like that, I think, how can she swim against the currents? Then I remember the note. She's Cassady, now. So maybe it's possible.

Regina Higgins has written a book on classic children's literature, Magic Kingdoms, published by Simon & Schuster. Her stories have been published in Rainbow Rumpus, Every Day Fiction, All Worlds Wayfarer, and Luna Station Quarterly. She lives in Lexington, Kentucky, and is currently writing a novel.

We will control the horizontal

TV reviews by Mark Bilsborough

Books can't constrain a good story, so why just look at words? This occasional TV and film column is going to take a closer look at what's happening on screen in our increasingly *Black Mirror* world, what we should be watching, and what we should avoid.

This time is all about what we should be watching, though. As we go to print we're midway through runs of *WandaVision* and *Snowpiercer*, and Amazon have just finished screening Season 5 of the *Expanse*, and that's as good a place as any to start.

The Expanse first. Based on a series of novels by James SA Corey (which is actually a couple of people, neither of them called James), *The Expanse* follows James Holden and his *Rocinante* crewmates through a series of near future adventures in the solar system and beyond. A few basic ideas drive the narrative: an alien 'protomolecule' has been discovered and weaponised by people way out of their depth, leading to tragic consequences. The protomolecule shapes and destroys and gains a form of sentience as it bonds with Julie Mao, daughter of one of the scientists working on taming it. By the time of *Expanse* season 5 the protomolecule has become a 'gate' which leads to thousands of other systems, many of them containing habitable planets. The 'Belters' control access to the gate – people who live in the asteroid belt, the outer planet and on the ships that fly between these settlements. There's conflict between the Belters and the 'Inners' (people from Earth and Mars, who are themselves in conflict) and it is this

dynamic that propels the action in this season.

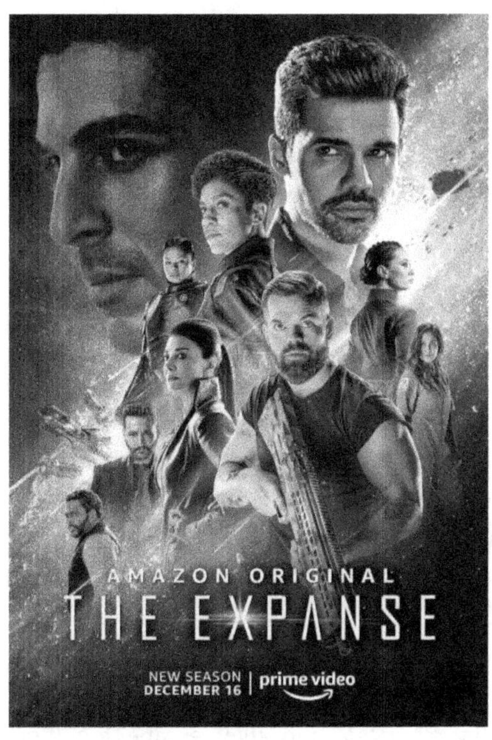

Each season is based on one of the source novels and this one's based on *Nemesis Games*, the fifth in the series. It's different from the others in that it takes the tight knit foursome from the stolen Martian gunship the *Rocinante* and fills in some backstory gaps. The protomolecule and the extrasolar planets take a back seat (back in focus next time, if the TV writers continue to follow the novels, but lurking in the background here) and the action focuses on Naomi Nagata – Belter and Holden's love interest – who is reunited with her long-lost son and forced to answer impossible questions about love and loyalty, Amos Burton, risking all to free Julie Mao's sister Clarissa from high security prison on Earth, and Alex Kamal, the pilot, returning to his home base on Mars to face up to his past.

Marco Inarios, Naomi's ex, is the leader of a miltant band of Belters who see an opportunity in their new found power as controllers of Gate access to strike at Earth, who he sees as the oppressors. His main weapon is to chuck rocks from the belt at Earth, with devastating consequences. He captures Naomi, reuniting her with their son, Filipe, who now associates with the militants. She escapes, only to find herself on a ship wired to explode when it approaches Holden and the *Rocinate*.

That's the main action, but I've always found the Amos Burton subplot the most fascinating part of this section of the *Expanse's* history. Burton's the brooding, taciturn one, full of many issues but little conversation. He heads back to Earth to confront his past – gangland in a decaying Baltimore – but also to rescue Clarissa Mao. She's in high security because she tried to destroy the *Rocinante* in the past, bent on revenge against the people (Holden etc) she felt were responsible for the death of her sister. But she bonded with Amos on the *Rocinante* and they escape together, finally ending back on the ship with Holden and Naomi.

This season is probably the strongest of the five so far, which is impressive because the book it's taken from, *Nemesis Games*, is arguably the weakest. It helps that we know the characters now, but I think this one works because it feels more grounded – a fight between different human factions without too much strange, conceptual alien distractions getting in the way means we can concentrate on the characters. Here, everyone except Holden has to face up to their past and refocus themselves. There are difficult choices to make across the

board and, right at the centre, Earth is devastated.

Plus, at the end there's an abrupt twist and a new direction to come. And something happens that's not in the books, which I'm a bit ambivalent about, and which I'll leave you to make your own minds up about. Always read the books first, that's a given, then watch *the Expanse* from beginning to now. Best science fiction on the television right now, IMHO, (and this coming from someone who loves *Star Trek Discovery* with a passion bordering on obsession).

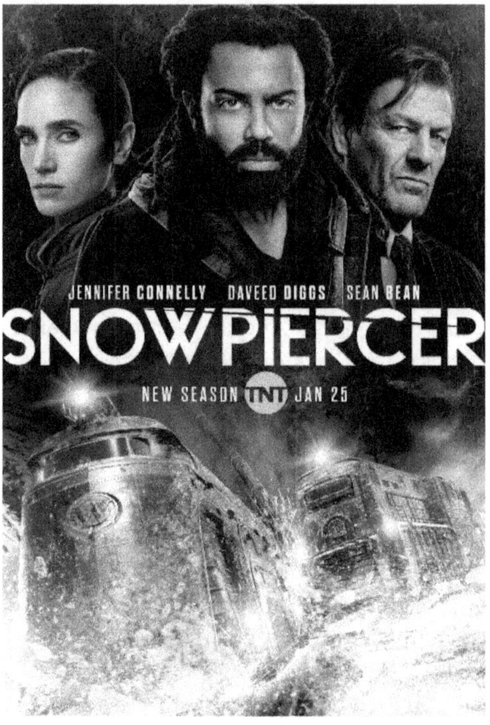

Also from a book is *Snowpiercer*, now in its second run, with a frankly silly premise. It's been filmed once, too, with Christian Bale being his usual moody self, so silliness clearly has never been an impediment to Hollywood spending money. Basic idea is that Earth is frozen over as a result of a misguided attempt to mess with the atmosphere to avert global warming, and all that remains is a 'perpetual motion' train about 1000 carriages long and holding

3000+ people. If they stop they freeze, so they trundle on around the world. The first season was all about the fight between the 'tailies' – (stowaways living in the baggage carriages) and the ticketholders in regimented classes. Democracy has prevailed by the start of season two and the tailies' hero Layton is in charge. Mister Wilford, the owner of the train, is revealed as being no longer aboard, presumed dead, with spokeswoman Melanie pretending he's in charge to preserve order.

But as Season One ends, Wilford is shown to be very much alive. He's been living on a supply train, Big Alice, which now connects with the main train. He's played by Sean Bean who's putting on his Posh Brit voice first seen in *Goldeneye* (so you know what to expect – English as last spoken in the 1950s with frequent lapses into pure Sheffield). He's not a nice man, our Mr Wilford, and his attempts to take over the main train make for some interesting tension, as does the dynamic between Snowpiercer's Melanie (former Wilford protegee now out to save the world) and her estranged daughter (brought up by Wilford and indoctrinated against the mother who 'betrayed' her) plus a bunch of other relationship issues around the crew and passengers. *Snowpiercer's* all about choice and betrayals, cruelty and compromise and this intense, little world is beautifully presented. This has become essential watching in the *Wyldblood* offices as counting down to the end of days becomes tinged with hope.

Which is more than can be said about *WandaVison*, Marvel's latest offering. Elizabeth Olsen and Paul Bettany play Avengers Wanda Maximov and The Vision respectively, opening in a small town *I Love Lucy* style sitcom, replete in black and white. But wait – isn't the Vision supposed to be dead? He was at the end of *Avengers*

Endgame (back in the days when we could see this sort of stuff in the cinema) but this is the comics, and no one stays dead for long. So because Wanda is the Scarlet Witch (though apparently only referred to by that name in the comics and not on screen) she can do magic, and she's created a little town-sized grief bubble for herself, playing a sitcom housewife with her newly reanimated dead android husband. And it's all beginning to unravel...

Marvel's film and TV arm (the MCU) is in danger of getting weighed down by its own complexity. It doesn't help that there's been no Marvel on the big screen since 2019 (for understandable COVID related reasons), or that this is the start of a new 'Phase' focusing on relatively minor characters (ie not Iron Man), Or that the storytelling here is complicated and relies on some pre-existing understanding of the characters. But somehow it works. Personally, I thought that the sitcom went on an episode or two too long before the narrative shifted into conventional Marvel gear, but now it has, this is genuinely intriguing, though I suspect you'd have to be a Marvel fan to start with to not be thoroughly confused.

My favourite part is when Wanda summons her long dead brother Pietro (Quicksilver) – because, er, because she can. But he's not played by the Quicksilver character from the MCU, killed in *Avengers: Age of Ultron.* Oh no! Instead we get the Quicksilver actor from the *X-Men* universe who used to do his thing for a rival film studio (Paramount – now taken over by Marvel parent Disney). I love it when it gets weird.

Which brings me to *Marvel's Agents of SHIELD*, which actually concluded a lifetime ago last August but is now rebroadcast in its shiny best on Disney+. *Agents of SHIELD* was always a bit silly but the last series was *profoundly* daft – an indulgent blow out from a creative team who knew that not only had the show been cancelled but it had been thrown out of the MCU which it was supposed to be tethered to. All because of control and continuity rows which were only ever going to be won by MCU Tzar Kevin Feige.

SHIELD former director Agent Coulson (killed in *Avengers: Assemble*) is on his third resurrection in this final season, in a robot body flying back through time (and across timelines) to stop series bad-guys Hydra

(the anti-SHIELD) from existing. Oh, wait, that's a bad idea because then *SHIELD* would never exist (since it was created to fight Hydra in the first place), so maybe it's about Hydra not getting too uppity. Or maybe it's about defeating the time traveling android Chronicons, who should be time lords but come across more like inept b-movie gangsters. Or maybe it's about the Inhumans, who Marvel were gearing up to be the mutants they no longer owned until Disney bought Paramount and they could play with the X-Men again. Bonkers from start to finish. Best series yet!

And the shows keep on coming. Golden age? You decide, but with new shows like Apple TV's alt-history *For All Mankind* (second series now running – Soviets get to the moon first) and more of Netflix's impressive fantasy series *The Witcher* and *Lost in Space* there's hardly enough time to get excited about *Star Trek: Strange New Worlds*. Disney's *the Mandalorian's* not my thing but I know someone must like it and there's another series on its way. And then there's the *Falcon and the Winter Soldier*, and possibly even some *Doctor Who…*

I should switch off and read something, but the screen is strangely compelling. What's that, Alexa? We will control the vertical?

Book Reviews
Mark Bilsborough

To Sleep in a Sea of Stars
Christopher Paolini,

In *To Sleep in a Sea of Stars*, YA writer Christopher Paolini's first leap into stories for an older audience, xenobiologist Kira Navarez gets more xeno than she bargained for as she unwittingly bonds with the alien Soft Blade, locked up for centuries for the galaxy's own protection by aliens that mankind is soon at war with. And before there's a second set of aliens in the fight, nightmares created, in part, from the Soft Blade itself. Can Kira defeat the nightmare Maw she feels responsible for and, in doing so, keep hold of her humanity?

All fantastic space opera – there are quirky characters, interesting shape-shifting aliens, an existential threat or two and plenty of battles in space. What works well a tight focus on Kira's character – I've never read a book this length with a single point of view character – and a boundless energy – but that's also a disadvantage because it robs the novel of depth and broad perspective. It helps, though, that Paolini has created a likeable and relatable character in Kira, though I think he's underwritten the psychological impact being bonded with an unpredictable alien symbiote might cause, particularly one that's killed your crewmates and your 'fiancé' (his words not mine. Is that a word people still use?).

What works less well is the sheer weight of this monster-sized book (and never have 881 pages felt this long). It literally took me weeks to read, and its fast pace often failed to sustain interest, particularly as many of the sequences were repetitive and plenty happens that, as one of my old writing instructors would be quick to point out, are very tangential to the causal chain. Plus there's hand wavey science, despite a technical appendix to explain it all (I skimmed that, just as I skimmed the others appendices and the acknowledgements).

I've never seen acknowledgements so long that they've had to be divided into part one and part two.) Plus some things aren't even hand-wavey – how do the underdeveloped 'nightmares', for instance, build their spaceships (they're supposed to be the creations of the angry/mad Maw without any science or history behind them) and why do they want to wipe out all intelligent life in the galaxy?

It's not a bad book, but it's not a good one either. Despite its plot shortcomings, the story at its core is engaging, but putting a box set into a single novel simply doesn't work for me and the occasional YA touches to the writing style irritate (for instance putting onomatopoeic words like *'crack'* in single sentences, like you tell schoolkids *not* to do). It's not that original, either. It feels like most of the key elements have seen an airing elsewhere. The subgenre doesn't really lend itself to originality because it has well defined tropes (space battles, maverick Captains, hostile aliens, symbiotes, surly, battle-hardened veterans with hearts of gold), all of which are visible here. But the best writers in the field make these ideas seem fresh. In addition, the aliens, sadly, aren't really well-developed; for the most part they remain the 'nightmares' or the 'jellies'. Maybe that will come in the (inevitable) sequel.

Then there's the ending. Hopefully not too spoiler-y to say it's implausible and (mildly) unsatisfying, and clearly designed to set up book two. I'm not sure I have the time or energy for that, though.

The Future of Another Timeline

Annalee Newitz

This is a solidly written, fast paced time travel story from the co-founder of the io9 website, Annalee Newitz. It's an intelligent, character-driven piece that just about manages not to trip itself up in time travel paradoxes.

Time travel stories are tricky because it's difficult to credibly imagine how causality might work. If you go back in time and kill your former self, for instance, how can you still be alive o go back in time to do the

deed? And – like the existence of aliens (obviously there are aliens but where are they?) – the absence of any proof of time travellers in the real world suggests there may be problems with getting it to work – after all, where were all the future people when the Titanic sank or Jesus was crucified?

Newitz' time travellers can change the world, but 'edits' work best in small ways – major changes are more difficult since the timeline snaps back. There's much discussion of the 'Great Man' syndrome – that one man such as Hitler can single-handedly change the course of history, and it's suggested here that wouldn't apply – without Hitler maybe Himmler or Goering or someone else may have taken the role – the times dictated the man rather than the man dictating the times.

There are two primary points of view. Tess, from 2022, and her old friend Beth, who in the initial timeline committed suicide in 1993. Tess, who was indirectly responsible for the suicide, profoundly changed after that incident (giving up, for instance, on being a moral-crusading serial killer) and (against the time travel rules) went back in time to save her friend. When she does, the event that had driven her whole later life is no longer present which gives her major cognitive conflicts – manifest in blinding headaches.

So this is partly Tess's story, about coming to terms with what she's done and who she is, and Beth's, negotiating a strained relationship with her parents, swerving a toxic friend and finding her way in life.

But it's also about a plot by future men – the Comstockers, latching on to real-life 19ᵗʰ Century ultra conservative outraged moralist Anthony Comstock – to deny women's rights across the timeline, specifically (but not exclusively) abortion rights. In the far future (which is hinted but not visited) some women are 'queens' who breed workers for the men in charge – and are routinely mutilated with their hands amputated in what appears to be a way to control and humiliate them.

Tess and her friends time travel by means of some ancient mechanisms embedded in rock in four parts of the world, discovered and used through the millenia. The machines make the rules – only on person at a time and you only carry clothes with you (ie no weapons). Though a future time traveller found a way to circumvent these restrictions. No going back to where you've been before as a time traveller, though you can cross your own natural timeline. No travel to your own future (though you can travel forwards to your own present from the time-travelled past).

These rules seem a bit arbitrary, but they do make the plot work. I liked the characters and the dual narrative (Tess/Beth and the Comstocker conspiracy) and I found the novel readable and engaging. Men generally don't come out well in this narrative, though, and I found some of its implications somewhat uncomfortable – it's certainly made me think about gender roles and biases. But I

liked its characters, its complexity and its spirit – a good read.

Curse the Day
Judith O'Reilly

I quite often get sent books which aren't really science fiction but which have some tenuous connection, as if that would tempt us genre folk in. This is one of them.

The sci-fi in *Curse the Day* is a McGuffin. A Skynet-style self-aware AI called Syd with no three laws of robotics to hold it back. End of the world, right? Except that the plot involves some crime and violence caper designed to *stop* Syd from breaking loose. And since the AI remains boxed in, the closest we get to anything not of this world is an automated kill zone in a London basement.

So this is definitely not science fiction (at least in my opinion). But is it a good crime book? It's got all the caper caricatures you could ask for – femme fatale, flawed hero (with a bullet in his brain as a unique and scarcely credible twist), cold, hard, ultra-attractive female assassin, annoying superbright teenage girl, corrupt, self-obsessed politician with a plot-convenient twin brother, violent but stupid general giant sidekick, distinctive, double-crossing ruthless boss (this one with one eye and an annoying smoking ritual), etc, etc – and the plot fair speeds along through one convoluted incident after another.

Michael North, an assassin who killed a lot of important people in a previous novel, is hiding out in Berlin when he gets the call to adventure and is repatriated to the UK hidden in a coffin (in an unnecessary action for action's sake sequence). He's recruited by the one-eyed man (Hone), who is high up in the Home Office, to protect his niece, Esme, who's married to computer genius and Syd inventor Tobias Hawke, who is about to set Syd free for reasons that aren't entirely clear. But then there's an attack at the British Museum where Hawke is about to reveal Syd to the world and Hawke is murdered. Who killed him? Will Syd break free? Will North forgive the cold-hearted assassin who killed his wife (and so, presumably, forgive himself for obviously fancying her)? And who (or what) is behind the mayhem that threatens teenage superhacker Fang's mum, Esme Hawkes life and the world-destroying rise of the machines (sadly only hinted – once with an overt Sarah Connor reference – and never explored)?

So lots for action fans who like broad brush characters and witty one-liners. It's great fun so long as you don't take it too seriously.

The Lost Colony
A G Riddle

This is the third in the *Long Winter* series by prolific science fiction author AG Riddle, who's been building a devoted fanbase with high action yarns. Recently he's been published in the UK by Head of Zeus, who have been developing a strong reputation for picking winners.

The *Lost Colony* doesn't really work as a standalone – as a reviewer we don't always get the choice to pick up at book one and, anyhow, books should work on their own, right? And I got suckered by this one – it's easy to pick up the flow for, maybe, two thirds of the book, then it hits you with material that will leave you absolutely scratching your head if you haven't read the other books. That's a shame, because I was well and truly sucked in by then, with the pace and the relentlessness of the twin narratives.

So I stopped reading *The Lost Colony* and worked my way through the first two books: *Winter World* and *The Solar War*, then came back to finish the last book (which by then make a lot more sense). This review, then, is inevitably (at least in part) a review of the series as a whole. Skip the next two paragraphs if you don't want spoilers for the first two books.

What's *Long Winter* all about? Well, in *Winter World* the earth is getting colder and colder, to the extent that glaciers are creeping all over the Earth. Incarcerated robotics genius James is sprung by a desperate team to investigate – and it's a space mission because a couple of weird artifacts have been discovered floating around where they have no right to be – blocking out the sun. And in the series' other point of view Emma is the sole survivor of the destruction of the International Space Station by forces connected to the artifacts. She's floating free in space – and James and his crew pick her up on the way to investigate the artifact. Communications attempts fail leading to war of sorts. It's pretty one sided – Earth freezes and mankind retreats to Tunisia and other (formerly) hot spots. But, led by James and Emma, the fightback begins…

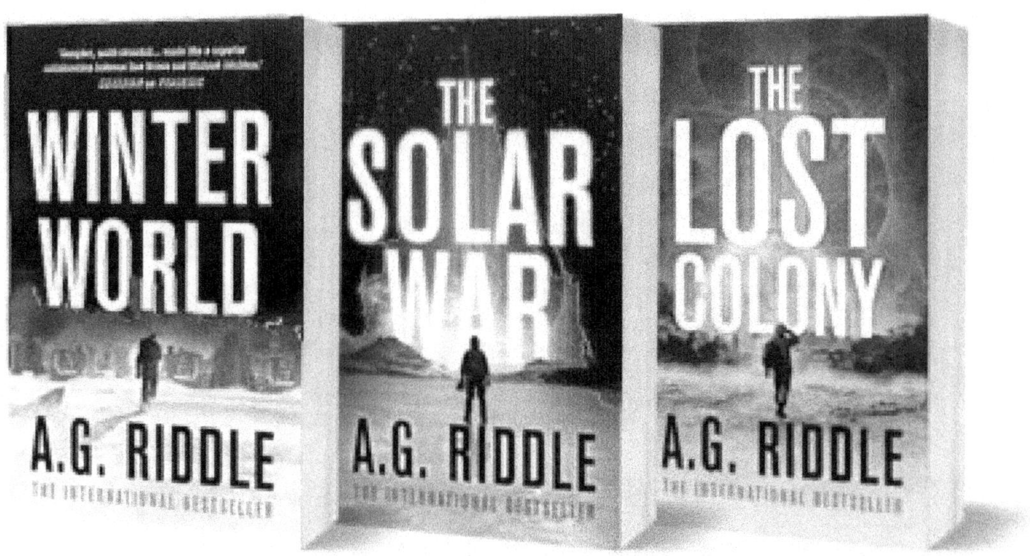

Book two has the aliens chucking rocks from the Kuiper Belt at Earth leading to the survivors (thousands out of billions) forced to contemplate a deal with the devil – or slow, chilly extinction. Eventually, they leave the uninhabitable Earth behind.

In book three the humans have regrouped on Eos, a tidally locked planet orbiting a red dwarf. But the planet, seemingly benign, has nasty surprises. The colonists can only live in valleys along the temperate band between boiling eternal day and freezing perpetual night. But a rogue planet periodically causes Eos to wobble, causing the temperate zone to shift into cold or hot – causing mass migrations of dangerous T-Rex type creatures – right through the colony. And – worse – retreating to the relative safety of caves causes its own problems – a pathogen with a 100% fatality rate. The only answer – stasis until a cure can be found. But Is the cure worse than the disease?

It's this point that stopped me short when I tried to read this book as a standalone (don't). And it's still weird going back to it. For one thing the writer's style changes completely. Up to that point in this book (though not the others) he's got the king of short sentences and short paragraph starting with conjunctions style of a hyperactive Dan Brown (though with admittedly better writing). But then the writing style gets much more conventional – and the story gets very confusing. There's a high concept at the heart of the series which is the cause of the confusion (at least with me), and which I found diverted from my enjoyment but I guess ramps up the SF credentials (as if the end of the world and colony planets weren't enough).

Still, these are easy and (in the main) satisfying reads. The first book is the best, but there's enough to keep a reader's interest across three volumes. But why stop there? Any chance of a fourth instalment?

And that's it – we hope you enjoyed our stories and features. Come and see us again in May for demons, robots and the pitfalls of negotiating your way around the virtual world.

www.wyldblood.com for orders and subscriptions.